A BLOW HOLE NOVEL

HAVING HOPE

NEW YORK TIMES BESTSELLING AUTHOR

TABATHA VARGO

TABATHA
Vargo

SEXY. SULTRY. SPICEY.

CONTACT TABATHA

www.tabathavargo.com
www.facebook.com/tabathadvargo
www.instagram.com/tabathavargo21
tiktok/@tabathavargoauthor
tabathavargowrites@gmail.com

Love and Death are two uninvited guests. Nobody knows when they'll come, but both do the same work ... one takes the heart, and the other takes its beat.

~Unknown

Prologue

A drunken haze settled over me, weighing me down and slowing my movements. I'd definitely had too much to drink, which wasn't uncommon for me ... especially at one of Finn's weekend parties. I could drink like a fish, smoke all the herb my lungs could handle, and Finn would always let me crash in his guest room.

My belt and jeans clattered to the floor. With so much alcohol swimming in my system, I'd struggled for five minutes to get them off. I ripped my shirt over my head, and my naked body collided with her naked body.

The girl beneath me had been bare for a while, while I'd kissed and licked every square inch of her. My body melted with hers when my arms finally gave in, and I collapsed on top of her completely, my full weight pressing her small frame into the mattress. Her skin was warm and soft, her fingertips soothing as they caressed my naked back.

"Please, Chet," she begged, her dark eyes looking straight into me.

I loved it when they begged, but her begging was different—more desperate—more frantic. She was both of those things because, unlike the rest of the girls, I'd taken my time to bring her close to orgasm and then let up for the last hour.

I didn't usually prolong a girl's release since giving pleasure was one of my favorite things. Hearing a woman moan and whine was probably the sexiest thing ever. But partying at Finn's place meant I could get fucked up and have a place to crash. So that was what I did.

Thanks to my alcohol and drug-induced total loss of control, I was weak and sloppy, which meant I had no choice but to take my time. I was sure I'd passed out twice while I made out with her, but my mind was so out of it I didn't care. This girl was something special ... something different, and I wanted to show her that.

It was more than that. It was the way she touched me. The way she'd treated me all night. She'd appeared out of nowhere because I'd never seen her at our parties. And she'd spent the night laughing and listening, not trying to stick her hands down my pants and grab my cock.

It was as if I was more than just a one-night stand for her, which would generally freak me out, but with her, it was different. She didn't push to sleep with me in the beginning. Instead, she'd talked to me and really laughed at my jokes, different from the fake bullshit most girls pulled. And I could remember her looking at me like I was more than the drummer.

Most girls wanted to fuck me because I was the drummer of Blow Hole, and the hotter the band got around town, the faster the women were. It was getting out of control.

No.

It was getting boring.

The chase was gone completely, but with her, I felt like I was chasing a bit. I felt like I was turning her on—like she wanted me for me—not because our band was on the verge of greatness. I liked the way she made me feel. I hadn't realized how much I missed just being Chet.

My hard cock lined up with her center, and her wet heat teased the tip. I looked down at her face, but the room around me spun, and I could barely see her dark hair and eyes through the blur.

She lifted her hips, and my body sank into hers. It was slow and felt beyond amazing, but it was harder to enter her than it should have been, considering how wet she was. There was a barrier, and I didn't miss her gasp when I finally pushed fully into her.

Something wasn't right. She was too nervous, her inexperience suddenly a glowing beacon in the dim room. Earlier in the night, her innocent noises and unsure touches had been endearing, but now, things were starting to make me wonder.

Her behavior wasn't the only thing that worried me. Her body gave her away. Regardless of how she'd been dressed at the party—her cleavage showing, her skirt short—her body told her secret. She was tight when I pushed into her. So tight and gripping at my cock that I thought I'd blow my load by entering her.

"Are you a virgin?" I slurred.

I was drunk. The fact that I was even noticing these things was crazy, considering I could barely see straight. The fact that I cared was even rarer.

"No. Don't stop," she whispered into the darkness.

I didn't want to stop. She felt better than any other girl had ever felt. Maybe it was because she was so tight and wet. Perhaps it was because we'd been touching and rubbing for the last hour. I wasn't usually much for foreplay, but I was so drunk and weak that lying against her and rubbing was easier than getting undressed.

"Are you sure?"

I didn't believe her. I hadn't been with any virgins. At least not that I knew of. And while people say that you couldn't feel the difference, I could. I could feel it in the grip of her body—the tenseness of her shoulders—the flashes of wide, nervous eyes that stared back at me.

She could say what she wanted, but she was definitely a virgin.

Still, if she wanted to pretend, then I could pretend, too.

"You feel so fucking good," I mumbled as I entered her again. "So tight."

I didn't fuck slow, but knowing that I was the first to break her barrier, I didn't want to hurt her.

That was definitely the vodka talking. Chet Rhodes didn't care about stupid shit like that, but with her, and after our drunken night together, I cared. I didn't want to hurt her. I wanted to make her feel as good as she was making me feel.

After an hour of making her body beg for release, it was the least I could do. Of course, I always made sure the ladies got off. It was the biggest reason they came back for the seconds I wasn't willing to give.

One time.

No more.

Otherwise, feelings reared their ugly heads, and I had nothing to offer anyone in that department.

She closed her eyes and swallowed hard, and then she dragged her nails down my back and pulled my hips to her. I sank into her tight passage again, and a moan rumbled up my throat.

"Fuck." My body went weak and fell entirely on top of her, my face buried into her neck.

She smelled sweet—like honey and vanilla—prompting me to lick her soft skin and taste her.

"Oh God," she breathed.

I moved into her, feeling an orgasm tease my balls. And when I was able to lift my head again, all I could see was the little blackbird inked into her ivory skin. I spent most of the night with my gaze glued to it. I couldn't look her in the eye because I knew I was drunk, so instead, I looked at the tat.

The blackbird moved with me, jumping with each thrust, taking flight with each of her deep breaths.

"Please don't stop, Chet," she begged.

I wasn't sure I could give her what she wanted. Already my shaft was hardening and preparing to unload. I wanted to come so badly, but at the same time, I wanted her to come, too.

I picked up my pace, my body still weak with vodka and everything else I'd downed during the night. My hips knew by memory what to do, so I continued to fuck her. The sensations were incredible.

"Come for me, baby."

What was her name?

Fuck!

How could I not remember her name?

Baby.

No.

Blackbird.

She'd be Blackbird from that moment on out.

My eyes stayed on the blackbird, and I picked up momentum the faster its wings seemed to flap. Her nails dug into my skin, and moans slipped from her lips with every breath. And then her body tightened around me, tugging sweetly at my throbbing flesh until I couldn't take it anymore.

"Oh my God," she said in shock, her eyes wide and unbelieving.

Obviously, no one had ever made her feel what she was feeling. It was a major boost to my ego and only pushed me harder to make her come.

"Yeah! Oh, yes!"

She cried out, her orgasm spilling from her body and gathering between us. The slapping sounds of our bodies coming together grew louder, echoing with the added moisture. The extra slide added to my pleasure; the sounds picked up as my drunken mind took the back burner, and my body's memory took over. My hips knew what to do. My body was in charge as I pounded into her, looking for my own release.

I fucked her hard and fast, filling her balls deep with each thrust. My spine went straight and stiff when the pleasure tightened my sack. And then I let go, coming inside her so hard no noise left my mouth. So hard my body went still as if I was being electrocuted by so much sensation. My mouth hung open. My eyes were glued to the blackbird as it became still.

Afterward, I rolled off her and pulled her to me so I could spoon her from behind. I wasn't a snuggly guy. Honestly, most nights, I asked them to leave, but with Blackbird, I wanted her next to me—holding me to the Earth and soothing me while I slept.

She moved, but I latched my arms around her and held her to me.

"Stay."

It was my voice. I'd asked her to stay. I could hardly believe it, but I knew what I wanted, and I wanted her. She melted into me, her body relaxing in the afterglow of our sex. I kissed her shoulder blade and ran my nose across her soft skin. Then the night moved over me, and I slept deeper than I had in months.

The following day, I woke with a splitting headache. My eyes were glued shut, and I was afraid to open them. The room spun behind my lids, and my stomach roiled with old vodka and beer.

Then the memories moved over me.

My night with her rushed through me, filling me with so much pleasure that I smiled through my throbbing brain.

We'd made out all night. I hadn't made out with a girl ... ever. We'd kissed and flirted—touched and teased—all the things I never did. We did all of this before going to the spare room at Finn's, where I spent an hour driving her crazy with my mouth and hands—prompting some of the sweetest noises I'd ever heard from her pouty lips.

Once she was squirming and begging for more, and once I wasn't sure I could hold myself together any longer, we moved past the foreplay and proceeded to have the best sex I'd ever had.

She was so tight—so wet—so perfect, and I knew I wasn't letting her out of my sight until I had her again. I wanted her over and over again. It wasn't like the other girls. She wasn't like the other girls. She was unique ... my little Blackbird.

She wasn't leaving the bed until I got a long sober look at her face, found out her name, and even snagged her number. She was different, giving herself to me in a way none of the other girls ever had. There were no sloppy seconds. I was the first, and strangely, I thought that maybe I'd like to be the last where she was concerned.

I'd never felt that way before, but my Blackbird had somehow chained me to her during our night together, and the thought of being a one-woman man for a bit didn't scare the shit out of me.

I rolled onto my side, reaching for her soft skin, ready to pull her to me and hold her close. My fingertips met blanket and blanket only. I patted at the sheets, reaching out farther, thinking that maybe she'd slept on the far side of the bed, but no one was there.

My eyes popped open as I sat up quickly. Nausea washed over me, and my head throbbed so hard I flinched. But worse than nausea and the pain was the realization that my Blackbird had taken flight at some point during the night, leaving only a tiny spot of her virgin blood on the sheets.

I couldn't remember her name.

I couldn't remember her face.

But I wanted her.

And if it was the last thing I did, I'd find her and make her mine again.

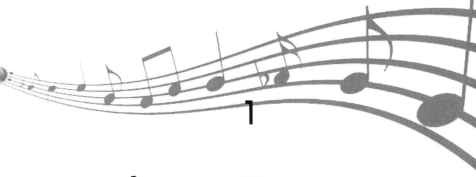

CHET RHODES
FIVE YEARS LATER

I was swimming in a sea of snatch. My body was plunging into it on a nightly basis as I attempted to cleanse myself in the sweet waters of a willing woman at every shot. I was engrossed in so much gash that all their features began to blur, swirling in my memories and becoming one unidentifiable face.

No specific hair color.

No exact eye shade.

No ideal body shape.

Women were everywhere—ready, willing, and sometimes begging to climb all over my stick. One minute, they were there, riding me and bringing me so much pleasure that I couldn't focus on anything around me, and the next, when it was over, they were gone. Discarding me like last night's stale clothes and moving on to something fresh.

So I did what any average red-blooded man would do.

I took advantage.

I indulged in their offers of release. Using their bodies to fill the void in my life and leaving them breathless with my experience and knowledge of the female body. Shutting out the world around me and forgetting the past that molded me so full of cracks and holes, I'd push myself inside another and disappear. Without fear of the future, I'd shut down and go into fuck mode without thinking.

It was my serenity.

It was my escape.

I've used this method ever since my younger days. Days far away in the back of my memory—days when the boys and I were playing hole-in-the-wall dive bars and scraping up change for smokes and the dollar menu at McDonald's.

I'd known then that women loved boys in bands. They wanted the lead singer's whispers against their flushed skin. They wanted the sweet vibrations of the bass player and the methodical fingering of the lead guitarist. But more than anything, they craved the drummer's stick—the beat of him pounding inside until they sang with pleasure—writing a melody of release all over me.

It was fucking beautiful.

I gave them what they wanted. I gave them the only thing I was capable of giving ... my body.

No deep emotional connections—no declarations of love or promises of more—only me and my cock. Only sex.

Then there was nothing.

Throughout the years of play—the many nameless, faceless women—only one thing stuck out in my mind. Only one thing made it to the forefront of my memories—shining through all my foggy recollections of fucking and forgetting.

A tiny blackbird nestled on perfect skin.

The tattoo stood out against her ivory complexion like a beacon for her memory. I'd close my eyes, and flashes of her tattoo would appear, shoving me back to the moment that defined me and the man I one day hoped to become.

Where that tattoo was located, I couldn't remember.

The only thing I remembered of what I'd deemed the best night with any woman was the blackbird. It was the only time I could remember going slow. The only time I took my time and melted with someone else—became one with a woman on another level.

The girl with the blackbird tattoo reached inside me—soothing internal scars—breathing life back into my decaying mind. She was an enigma—a dream—but she existed. I had no doubt in my mind that night had happened. Everything about her was real.

I was young. I was high and drunk out of my mind. Therefore, I didn't remember much about her, but I did remember the tiny tattooed salvation. The symbol of freedom, which remarkably reminded me of the way she'd made me feel that night.

Not a day went by that I didn't think about my Blackbird. I couldn't remember her face—her smile—nothing. I only remembered the feeling of someone truly wanting me for me and no other reason. I wasn't the drummer of Blow Hole. I was Chet Rhodes, and she looked inside and saw *me*.

I went to sleep next to her, wearing a smile of relief for the first time in my entire life, thinking when I woke, she'd still be there, and I'd possibly found the one who could lock me down. But when I woke the following day with a raging headache and a sick stomach, she was nowhere to be found.

I hated myself for getting so fucked up that I couldn't remember specifics, and I'd continue to hate myself. Until her and after her, they were the same woman—all the same, everything—nothing like my Blackbird.

That was my before.

She was my past and my biggest regret. I didn't regret that she had happened. I regretted that she had gotten away so easily because I was too fucked up to keep it together.

Fucked up was how I lived then. Things were rough in the beginning—the only good in my life had been the girls and the tiny bit of fame we'd earned back home in South Carolina.

Everything else about my existence had been the thing of nightmares. I never let on to the guys, but I'd slept on a park bench with nowhere else to go many nights—the cool night air stinging my skin and the hard metal of the bench leaving me stiff.

The guys were my family—my brothers—my support. They had been since the moment I came home to our piece of shit trailer to find it empty.

No furniture.

No pictures.

No mother.

What kind of person packed up everything and left her son while he was at school?

Who could do something so fucked up?

My mother.

That was who.

Thankfully, the bitch left my shit on the front porch. I had my clothes and a few pieces of my past, and that was all until the moment we signed our contract.

That was then.

These days, we were living the glamorous life. After signing a major record deal, we had more money than we could blow.

Trust me.

I'd tried.

I'd spent many weekends with the white rabbit running up my nostrils, and the cocaine afterglow dripping down the back of my throat, numbing me from the inside out and frying my regrets and memories. I'd smoked more herb than my rattling lungs could contain, and I'd drunk enough booze to drown an Irishman.

Some days, I'd wake up with my head spinning and my stomach heaving—days I'd find myself surrounded by sleeping strangers with no memory of the night before—no memory of anything. Only tangled, naked limbs and the smell of sex to wake me.

That was my life.

My jam.

It was the only way I knew how to survive—to keep the truth hidden and the darkness at bay. If I didn't, it would choke me. If I didn't keep it hidden, I'd live each day thinking about my last day, and I couldn't do that. Instead, I lived without care, without knowing when that day would be.

I'd grown accustomed to that way of life.

It was fucking beautiful.

It was everything a young, carefree man like myself could ever want.

The boys and I were living the lives of kings, and then everything went away.

My boys were plucked off one by one, finding true love and starting families and shit.

Things were changing. Things were growing ... evolving. The boys weren't down for a good party anymore. They wanted more, and I couldn't blame them for that. They were receiving the things that I could only dream of.

Zeke, our lead guitarist, was the first. He had fallen for a tiny blond with so much heart and love to offer it was sickening. They had kids together ... beautiful blond girls who thought I was the funniest person on Earth.

Patience and Zeke were perfection together, and even though I never thought Zeke would settle down, Patience had captured him and locked him down ... happily. I'd never seen him really smile, and I'd known him for years, but these days, he smiled all the time with Patience.

Finn, our lead singer, followed behind Zeke, running into his first and only love again only to find out they had a son together. He was a changed man from that moment on. And they made a home together and brought a daughter into the world.

To see our leader, the man who never broke for anything, fall so hard and be so completely wound up over a woman was hilarious. I couldn't say I understood it, but the happiness on his face every time he saw his wife, Faith, made it easier to accept.

And then there was Tony, aka Tiny, who was marrying the daughter of a rock legend. They started out bumpy, drugs and their pasts getting in the way and keeping them apart, but their love was obvious, and I was happy for him and Constance. I knew it wouldn't be long until they, too, were popping out babies and living the family lifestyle.

I didn't hate them for deciding to settle down and become family men.

Not really.

I loved my nieces and nephew, and while I ragged the boys hard for being domesticated pussy boys, I was jealous of all the things they were gaining in their lives—things much bigger than a record deal—much better than the fame and money.

My boys were growing loving families, and I knew I could never have that. I would never shackle a woman to me. It would be wrong to do so since I had nothing to offer but a lifetime of pain and worry ... a lifetime left of suffering.

So as I stood by Tiny's side and played the part of his best man, I knew I was losing more than my final wingman. I was losing more than our nights partying at the condo we'd once lived in together in California. I was losing the last ounce of hope that maybe I wouldn't die alone.

Tiny was moving on. He'd found the one who filled his dark corners with light—the one who made breathing through his demons a little bit easier—and no matter how sad I was to be losing him, I was happy for him.

I was happy for all of them.

Standing beside my boys, all dressed in our wedding wear of suits and bowties, I looked across at the girls of Red Room Sirens and grinned. Tiny was marrying their lead guitarist—he was locking his life to hers—and I approved. I liked Constance and already considered her family.

She was beautiful—hardcore and a hard-ass, which was precisely what Tiny needed. She was tall and blond, a perfect match for Tiny and his large, muscular frame. She smiled up at him as he said his vows, and the look in her eyes—the absolute love that I could see swimming in her emotions—left an aching sensation in my gut.

I'd never know that.

I'd never have that look directed at me.

Never.

Shaking my thoughts and clearing my throat, I let my attention settle on the stars of the show.

Tiny and Constance.

I wished them so much happiness, which I knew they'd have, and I silently cursed the devil in the back of my mind for taking away my chances for the same.

My eyes moved down the line of bridesmaids, leaving Constance and landing on their lead singer, Lena. She stood tall, her eyes glistening with unshed tears. Feeling my gaze on her, she looked my way and grinned. I gave her my signature smirk, making her shake her head and turn away.

The girls of Red Room Sirens had grown accustomed to my flirty ways. After two months together on the Rock Across America tour, we had grown close. We spent time together, and they began to understand me the way my boys did. They knew what I was about, and in some strange way, I think they understood and respected my decision on how I chose to live my life.

These beautiful girls became my friends, which was a first for me. I didn't have female friends, but after some time with them, I found myself not looking at their tits as much. Not thinking about fucking them.

They were different from the rest of the girls I knew. They were untouchable, worth more than a one-night roll in my bed. And when they smiled at me, I knew it was because they felt the same about me.

Except for one.

Hope, the drummer for Red Room Sirens, was the strangest woman I'd ever met.

She wasn't sexy in the usual sense. Actually, she was awkward and unfriendly. She dressed unlike any other girl I knew and rarely smiled. She'd show up to rehearsal some days wearing cartoon pajama bottoms, a top that didn't match, and combat boots.

Weird.

But something about her carefree attitude and thrown-together style made her attractive. She was short and trim; her shoulder-length hair weaved with rainbow strands, and her eyes were so dark the blackness threatened to steal away any light shining near her.

Her laughter was contagious—loud and as unique as her style—but rare. Emotion of any kind wasn't something I imagined Hope showed. She was unreadable. Her young face was like stone—expressionless and hiding what I guessed was a dark past—until she picked up her drumsticks and played.

Then she transformed, becoming transfixed on the beat. She lost herself so beautifully in the music that I couldn't look away when I watched her play. Only then did she wear a genuine smile. Only then was I able to glimpse the light within her.

Her smile changed her appearance completely, and she went from strange and unusual to sweet and friendly in seconds. It was sad she didn't smile more often because she went from detrimental beauty to soft and approachable with just a simple tilt of her pouty lips.

The oddest thing about her wasn't her awkward sense of style or the hidden shadows in her eyes that only another broken soul could see. It was the fact she obviously hated me, and I had no fucking clue why.

She wasn't shy about it at all. Her disdain for me showed in her expression every time she looked at me. Disgust would consume her sweet face, and her cheeks would redden with what I could only assume was anger.

She made it a point to stay away from me during the entire tour. She barely looked at me, and her lips would curl in contempt when she did. She rarely spoke to me, but she was full of attitude and hatred when she did. And being the sick fuck that I was, I loved every fucking second of it.

Women threw themselves at me. They generally liked me and liked that I was able to make them laugh. They enjoyed that I could thrill them for a night since most women were always looking for a way to leave reality. I could give them that while I rocked them all night long.

Hope obviously didn't give a fuck about any of that.

She wasn't anything like other women—whether they were my Red Room friends or the women I fucked—and it drew me to her. It made her interesting, and I watched her a lot because of that.

I couldn't figure her out, and I needed to know what made her tick. I wanted to know why the shadows danced behind her hatred, but I never pushed. I let her stay away and kept my distance, as well.

As my eyes landed on the woman in my thoughts, her lips went from unexpressive to tilting down in disgust. I could tell by her expression that she could feel my eyes on her. I chuckled at her frown and quickly smacked a hand over my mouth. Tiny turned my way with confusion in his eyes before continuing with the ceremony.

Hope turned away from Tiny and Constance and looked at me. As usual, her lips curled, and her eyes narrowed. I loved it. I loved every fucking second of her hatred. It was legit. Tangible. And for some reason, I respected her more because of it.

Her gaze dipped to my smiling lips, and she turned away, rolling her eyes. And right there, in front of everyone watching, my cock grew.

It was sick.

Disgusting.

Demented.

But that was the kind of guy I was.

I was stiff and ready to go, standing in front of a group of people while my best friend got married, but I didn't care.

Everyone knew me. I didn't hide my freak. Fuck it. I let my dick stand tall against the black slacks.

I wouldn't fuck with Hope because I usually didn't shit where I ate. As far as Hope was concerned, she was now a part of my home since her bandmate was marrying my bandmate. But it was more than that. Not only was I sure she'd try to kill me if I tried to get in her pants, but Tiny and Constance getting married meant the girls of Red Room Sirens were officially off-limits ... as in, no dipping my stick in their sweet spots.

That didn't mean I didn't fantasize about Hope and her tiny claws digging into my skin. It didn't mean I didn't think about wrapping my long fingers around her delicate neck and squeezing as I made her come repeatedly.

She would be wild in bed—a freak like me—ready and willing to do anything and everything. Just thinking about all the positions I could put her in—all the things she'd be down for—was almost too much. But I would never go there with her.

It was wrong. It would form a chasm between the Sirens and the boys when shit went sour between us, which it definitely would. I didn't fuck the same girl twice, and no matter how emotionless Hope seemed, she was still a woman. Women tended to get attached. Putting a hole between Blow Hole and the Sirens was the last thing I wanted to do.

That didn't mean I wouldn't flirt my ass off for the fun of seeing her disgusted expression. It didn't mean I wouldn't sneak in little touches here and there so she'd claw at my hand in rage. I was easily amused, and Hope's open hatred of me was amusing.

After the I dos and the blur of Tiny signing his life away, I found the redhead I'd spotted sitting in the back eye fucking me and took her somewhere a little more private.

I was a fucking wreck. I was losing my boys ... my family. And while they were gaining their lives, I never gained anything permanent for myself. I didn't want to think about it.

I needed to lose myself in something wet and ready, and the redhead was both of those things.

Red on the head meant fire in the hole. The redhead I was fucking against the bathroom wall of the luxury resort where Tiny got married was a spitfire. She ripped at my skin with her pointed nails and bit my shoulders. All while begging me to fuck her harder.

When I was finished with her and leaving the bathroom to go back to the reception, I was no longer thinking about my future and what I'd never have. Instead, I focused on the present and everything I did have.

I was a fucking rock star. I had the world at my fingertips, and I planned to take advantage of that for as long as possible.

2

CHET

After the wedding reception, I drove around Los Angeles and took in the sights. The radio blared Avenged Sevenfold, and I played the drum sections on my steering wheel with my palms. The palm trees on the side of the road blurred as I sped down the lane, becoming one brown and green mass of nothingness.

We had lived in California for a while, but we worked so much that we rarely got to see the city we lived in. It felt like a good night to get to know the strange place I'd moved to with my band. I didn't love California. It could never be South Carolina … it could never be home, but it was what I had—it was where my boys were—and so it was where I'd stay.

I kept driving, running the gas out in my car and trying to get my thoughts together. I wasn't ready to return to the condo alone. Technically, the place was mine now. The boys had moved out, living the family life, and now, Tiny was joining their ranks. But the condo was huge, with more bedrooms than I'd ever use, a gym I'd never stepped foot in, and three living room spaces.

Overwhelming for a single man like myself, I tried to make sure to fill the place every chance I got to stave off the fact that I was virtually alone in the world. If I had to party every night to numb my loneliness, I'd do it. I'd do whatever it took to forget my circumstances.

That was what I did.

It was who I was.

After driving for a few hours, I finally went home. The first thing I did when I went inside was to go to the freezer and pull out my trusty bottle of vodka. I hadn't drunk much at the reception since I knew I had to drive home, but that didn't mean I couldn't get shitfaced at home alone.

Ripping the bowtie from around my neck, I stripped down to my boxers as I made my way into the living room and collapsed onto the leather sectional with a smack.

Taking a long swig from my bottle, I lay back on the couch and stared up at the unique overhead lighting that shined down on me. It was some contemporary bullshit the designer for the condo had put up. I hated it. I had since the first night we stayed there, but at least it wasn't a shitty trailer in a dangerous trailer park.

Thirty minutes and half the bottle of vodka later, the room spun, and I chuckled to myself. Drinking alone wasn't a good thing. My mom used to drink alone, and everyone in the neighborhood knew she was an alcoholic. I'd never be that way, but this night was different. I was drinking alone as an official sendoff for my boy Tiny.

My eyes grew heavy, and the light above me began to blur as sleep moved over me and threatened to claim me for the rest of the night. I was almost gone when I heard the front door open and slam. Seconds later, I opened my eyes to find Finn standing with his arms crossed.

Finn was the lead singer of Blow Hole, but he was so much more. He was our ringleader and the oldest of our chaotic group. He'd taken on the big brother role and always ensured we had our shit together and were on time for everything.

He stayed on top of us for years, making sure we didn't accidentally kill ourselves by overindulging, but these days, I was the only one he felt he needed to worry about. He was my family—my brother—and I loved him.

He was bigger than I was, taller and more muscled and broad across the shoulders like a linebacker. The ladies loved him and his smooth rhythmic voice, thinking he was walking sex, but I knew differently. Finn was smart and capable with a damn good head on his shoulders.

He always did the right thing, which meant he denied all the crazy and focused on the ones he loved the most ... his wife and kids, us boys, and his mom, who had also given me a place to lay my head many nights after my mother had hauled ass.

"You good?" he asked.

I nodded, the room slowly coming into focus as my eyes settled on Finn. "Yeah, man, I'm good. What's up?"

"Nothing much. Zeke thought it might be a good idea to come over and make sure you were still breathing." He fell onto the couch across from me and sighed. "Shit's getting weird, huh?"

I chuckled. "Shit's been weird for a long time. It's good, though. It's life, man."

I leaned up, shook the dizziness away, and started to roll a blunt on top of the coffee table.

"Yeah, I guess so," he agreed. "We're all settling down. Who would've thought that would've ever happened?"

I nodded before bringing up the blunt and licking it to seal it.

"Not me, but everyone's gotta do it at some point."

The room went quiet, only the sounds of my lighter and the crackling tip of my blunt filling the space. Finn's eyes never left my face.

"What about you?" Finn asked.

I inhaled, the smoke burning my lungs until they ached.

I exhaled and coughed.

"What about me?" My voice was strained and broken from the smoke.

"When are you going to settle down? Find a nice girl and have some kids and shit."

I couldn't help myself.

I laughed.

Hard.

"Come on, man. You know that shit's never going to happen." I shook my head.

"Why not?"

He was being serious.

I'd known Finn for a long time. We'd met in high school, him being a few grades ahead of me before he finally quit. He'd been through some crazy shit. We all had. But still, I couldn't bring myself to tell Finn the real reasons behind my solitude.

No one knew.

And that was precisely how I wanted to keep it.

I wouldn't burden anyone with that bullshit.

"It's not for me, man. You boys are settled. All married with kids and shit. And that's great for y'all. Marriage looks good on y'all, but it's just not for me. I wouldn't know what to do with the same woman every night, and while I love the kids, I could never have any of my own."

Not because I didn't want any, but because it would be wrong to procreate when I knew I couldn't take care of them. I wouldn't lock a woman with my baby and leave her hanging like that. My own mother and father had abandoned me. I knew how badly that shit sucked.

Finn nodded his understanding and let it go. I was glad. I hated deep thoughts and long heart-to-heart talks. I especially hated it when I was drinking and smoking because I was more likely to spill all my business.

He took the blunt when I handed it to him. It was rare that Finn ever smoked anymore. Ever since he'd found out he had a son, he'd slowed his rock 'n' roll lifestyle. Kids did that to you, I guess. Zeke had been the same, and I was sure once Tiny knocked up Constance, he would too.

It wouldn't be long before I was utterly alone with everything. I'd been born alone. I'd grown up alone. And one day, I'd die alone. Death was inevitable, but life was a choice. I chose to live every day like it was my last.

Finn stayed for an hour shooting the shit. We laughed about some bullshit that went down at Tiny and Constance's wedding and went over some lyrics for the next album, but when Faith called and told him the baby wouldn't stop crying, he grabbed a water bottle out of the refrigerator and left.

His wife.

The baby.

The boys had wives and kids.

I had nothing.

I never would.

I'd never cared about all of it before, but the older I got, the more the ideas bounced around in my head. And the more the ideas bounced around in my head, the more I had to squash them and remember my predicament.

That night, I passed out on the couch instead of going to my room. My sleep was disturbed, my body stretching and reaching to get away as a flock of blackbirds attacked me in my nightmare.

I dreamed about blackbirds a lot. They symbolized a simpler time in my life. They reminded me of when I didn't have anything to worry about except my next high and when to show up for practice. But more than that, they symbolized the sense of peace I hadn't been able to capture since that night five years before.

The night I stepped away from the guy I was and settled into the man I wanted to be. The night I changed, only to wake up to my reason gone and eventually slip back into my old ways.

The tiny Blackbird was gone and never returned.

She was my peace.

She was my sanctuary.

And the bits and pieces of her memory and the regrets I held on to for letting her go were slowly trying to kill me. And I was going down without a fight.

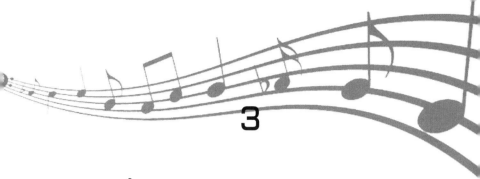

3

HOPE IVERSON

What could I say about **Chet Rhodes** that every woman in the world wasn't already thinking?

He was ridiculously gorgeous in an annoying I-really-want-to-ride-his-face-but-also-stab-him-in-the-eye kind of way.

His tall, lean frame towered over most women, and his dark, knowing eyes could somehow see right through you. I was convinced he always knew what I was thinking, and I fucking hated that since, more often than not, I was imagining his hands all over me.

He shaved the sides of his head but left long, unmanageable strands on the top. It was a Mohawk, but it wasn't. All I knew was it hung in his eyes a lot, giving him a sexy, mysterious look, and every time I looked at him, I longed to push my fingers through it.

Every inch of his body was tattooed ... at least the parts you could see, which was a lot if you'd ever been to a Blow Hole concert. Chet had no shame and was quick to strip naked behind his drums if he got overheated. I didn't blame him there. Being on stage beneath the beaming lights was hot as fuck. Add in the constant jamming on the drums, and you had yourself a hell of a workout.

He had piercings. His left eyebrow had a hoop, and he had silver snake bites beneath his bottom lip that drew your attention straight to his luscious mouth. His ears were gauged, but not too much, which I could appreciate, and his tongue piercing instantly made me wonder what the little silver ball would feel like against my clit.

Constance had once hinted that his dick was pierced, too, which I didn't doubt, but that was one piercing I'd never see, and that was fine by me.

Basically, Chet was fucking sexy. Sadly, he was aware of this, and much to my dismay, every woman I could think of agreed with that assumption. But none of that mattered to me because I could say without batting an eye that I hated Chet Rhodes with a passion that burned hotter than the fires of hell.

I'd never hated anyone before, except for a few assholes I'd gone to high school with who told the entire school I was a good lay. But with Chet, it was unavoidable. I had to hate him because not only was he annoyingly sexy and the biggest dog I'd ever had the unfortunate chance to meet, but also because the motherfucker didn't remember me.

I realized he didn't remember me the first time I saw him again at the beginning of the Rock Across America tour. He looked right over me without even a drop of familiarity. He looked through me like I was fucking invisible—like I wasn't breath, blood, and bones before his eyes—like he hadn't given me the best night of my life when I was younger.

I was at a loss.

For years, I'd conditioned myself not to feel anything. I'd taught myself to ignore the strange aches that formed in the pit of my stomach or the sadness that laced everything in life, but the second his eyes passed over me and I realized he didn't recognize me at all, my heart imploded, sucking away all my oxygen with it.

At that moment, my hatred for Chet Rhodes began.

The fucked-up part was I hadn't really changed all that much over the years. I was still the same girl he'd entered slowly. The same girl he'd spent the night with, whispering sweet nothings in my ear in his sleep. I was the same fucking girl. Except for different hair colors and less provocative clothing, I was unchanged.

I was older and wiser—more mature—more aware of how stupid I used to be. I was no longer the young girl dressing in revealing clothes in the hopes of catching the attention of the sexy drummer. That girl died years ago, and she was never coming back.

He looked me over. His eyes passed over my sleeveless T-shirt and ripped jeans before settling on Mia, our bass player, with her thick thighs and giant, overflowing tits.

I'd never felt so inconsequential. I'd never felt so minuscule, which said a lot since I'd been placed on the metaphorical back burner most of my life—left to simmer and burn until nothing was left of me.

I wasn't surprised. I'd always known nothing was special about me. I knew nothing made me stand out among the hordes of other women.

But knowing our night together had changed me so irrevocably and hadn't affected him at all sucked. Knowing that our night together had altered the girl I'd once been so thoroughly, yet he obviously had no memory of me and our time together whatsoever burned in the place where my heart and soul had once settled.

All the time I'd wasted stressing once we received our invite to join the Rock Across America tour. All the nights I'd spent awake worried about us seeing each other again once the Rock Across America tour started. All the replaying possible explanations for my sudden disappearance in case he asked.

It was all for nothing.

Nothing.

None of it mattered because I was just another wet hole for him to lose himself in and never think about again.

It was ignorant of me to assume he still thought about me. It was dumb to think he spent the last five years wondering why I'd left without saying goodbye.

Did he even care if he ever saw my face again?

How could he not fucking remember me?

Then again, we're talking about Chet Rhodes. The famed drummer for Blow Hole, he was the biggest man whore in America. But he was also the man who stripped me bare emotionally and took the innocence I so readily gave to him.

I didn't know the kind of man he was back when I'd dressed provocatively in hopes of gaining his attention. I didn't know he was a hit-it-and-quit-it kind of guy, even though everyone else knew—even though he made it clear to all his conquests—I didn't know. I was too young and stupid to understand.

All I cared about was his playing and how amazing his happy smile was. All I thought about was getting to know him better and maybe learning a few of his drumming techniques. I didn't realize I'd developed feelings until it was all said and done.

If I had known who he really was, I would have never let him climb between my virgin thighs. If I had known what I was walking into and the consequences, I would have never let myself fall and become so attached.

But I had, and I'd spent every day since regretting it. I spent every moment since in a constant state of sadness and anger. Always trying to forget but never being able to.

So when I saw him again, and his eyes moved over me without even an ounce of acknowledgment, my hatred formed. Every day, it deepened. Every day, I despised everything about him even more.

His smiles—the way he eyed the women in the crowd—I hated every fucking thing about him. By the time the Rock Across America tour was over, I could barely contain myself and my obvious disgust for Chet.

Some days, I wanted to go to him and explode like a fucking grenade, taking him down with me. When the girls would force me to go around the boys of Blow Hole, I would drink until my face went numb. I'd hope my anger would consume me, and I'd grow the balls to put my fist through his perfect face.

I didn't do any of those things, though. Instead, I kept it all in—never telling a single soul about my past—letting it slowly fester until I knew any good left within me had rotted to black. Ash and soot that weighed me down.

It was the strangest thing. Spending two months on tour with Blow Hole and some of the biggest bands in the industry should have been the best thing that ever happened to me, but it wasn't. It was the hardest thing. It was soul-crushing, and I found myself overthinking everything and slacking on my drums.

It fucking sucked.

Still, I couldn't complain too much. Other than the craziness with my past and Chet, life was good.

Red Room Sirens, the all-girl band I played drums for, had two top ten hits, a third album in the works, and performed in part of the biggest rock tour in America. We'd come together—all girls with different backgrounds—and we made music that kicked ass. We rocked harder than the men we toured with—giving it our all at every show—and earned the respect of the other bands.

For the first time in my life, I wasn't living for the day. I wasn't worried about finding food or a place to lay my head at night. Growing up was rough. Having parents who cared more about their high than their child made me tougher than most, but I'd lived hard. I'd cried harder. And I'd survived some of the biggest losses a person could go through.

Thanks to my love of the drums, I'd made a career for myself. All I could do was hope that my lucky streak would continue, but I wasn't foolish enough to think that everything couldn't get sucked away just as quickly as it came into my life.

I had money.

I had food.

And I had clothes to keep me warm.

I'd gotten all of that without my abusive piece of shit father. I'd climbed to the top without my alcoholic mother. I'd gotten it all on my own with the help of my new family ... the Sirens.

Still, being around Chet Rhodes had been pure torture.

So every day, I stewed. Every day, my resentment for everything he'd stripped from me grew. And every day, I lived in miserable silence, hoping and praying that he wouldn't remember me. It hurt, him not remembering, but at the same time, it made me less anxious. I stayed away from him, and after a few weeks, he learned to stay away from me.

It was easier that way.

"I can't believe Constance is married," Lena said as she climbed into the back of the limo.

She was a California girl. They all were. I was the out-sider—the Easterner—the Southerner. I'd taken seven buses to get to California all those years ago, and I'd slept on every bench in Los Angeles until Gary Steele found me tapping my drumsticks on a statue at a local park.

That was how I was discovered.

Dirty.

Hungry.

Angry.

And beating the shit out of a rhythm on a statue that reminded me of my father.

"I know. Shit's crazy," I agreed.

I scratched at the silky fabric of my bridesmaid's dress. I couldn't wait to get home and rip it from my body. I wasn't the kind of girl to wear such things. I was a ripped jeans and hoodie kind of girl. I was a sweats and tank girl. The girlie dresses and heels bullshit was for the birds. Give me my boots and Converse any day.

I tapped my drumsticks against my thigh to the rhythm of our latest song. Album number three was proving to be my favorite so far. I could hear our growth when we played, and the drum solos let me expand on the sound. I'd even put down some lyrics with Constance—letting out some steam lyrically and secretly ripping Chet and everything he stood for apart.

"Hopefully, things don't change too much. We just stepped on the scene. Things are just now starting to look up for us," Mia said with closed eyes as she rested her head against the back of the seat.

"That won't happen. Tiny lives this life, too, which means touring, and all the shit that comes with our career won't get in the way. Constance and Tiny work. We shouldn't think about anything else. We should be happy for them," Twiggy said.

We all agreed.

Let Constance enjoy her two-week honeymoon because when she got back, it was time to go to work. Let her enjoy the life I knew I'd never let myself live.

Settling down wasn't an option. I couldn't give someone something I didn't have. I could never hand over my heart and love to someone the way they deserved. I'd given my heart away years before. I'd set it in the hands of a virtual stranger and watched as he walked away with it.

Now, my life mirrored Chet's, sadly. Except where he fucked anything that moved because I didn't sleep around. The girls thought I did. At times, I'd purposely go off with a guy and leave him once we were away from the girls. They thought I was wild, sleeping with any man or woman I wanted, but the truth was, I was afraid.

I knew the consequences of such actions, and I would die alone if it meant protecting myself against everything, including heartbreak. It was the only way I could imagine living. Any other way wasn't safe. Any other way hurt too much.

The girls dropped me at my apartment after the reception. I went into the lonely space that I'd made my home, showered, and crashed. I slept for shit, and once the sun burst through my sheers, I gave up and climbed from my bed.

23

My apartment was spacious. Only two bedrooms, it was plenty for me. I didn't have much when I rented the place—just a single bag full of my personal belongings—but over the last year, I'd added furniture and even hung a few pictures of the girls and me.

In the kitchen, I scrambled two eggs and ate standing at the counter. The place was quiet—lonely—but at least it was mine. It was the only real home I'd ever known. I didn't need people or their affection and love. I only needed my freedom, my drumsticks, and a roof over my head. The rest could squat in my memories and eat me from the inside out.

Constance came back from her honeymoon two weeks later. We went straight to work on our third album, spending most of our time in the studio. Staying busy was a great thing for me. As long as I was working, I didn't have time to dwell on anything outside the studio.

My mental state flourished. The more days that passed after the Rock Across America tour, the less I thought about Chet. The more I worked and focused on the music, the less I thought about my past and everything I'd lost. Things were looking up, and the more we worked on our latest album, the more I knew it would be our best yet.

"That shit sounds so good," Finn praised.

It wasn't often, but on occasion, Tiny and Finn would stop by and listen. I'd never get over hearing praise from Finn but agreed the sound was solid, and I knew our fans would love it.

I smiled as I watched them outside the recording booth nodding their heads to my beats. Having the respect of the Blow Hole boys meant a ton to us.

Minus Chet.

Of course.

He could go suck on a sweaty sack as far as I was concerned.

We wrapped the album a month later and started promotion with the label soon after that. Life fell into its own rhythm. I'd work, spend time with the girls, and then I'd go home to my lonely apartment and dwell on the past.

It wasn't healthy, but nothing about my lifestyle was.

The drugs.

The drinking.

The inner anger and rage.

I used those things to drown out the cries from my past. It was my way to forget all the stupid decisions I made. Living my life busy and out of control kept me sane, which mattered more than my physical health.

Men pushed themselves on me. They all wanted a piece of the drummer. Some women even tried to get a piece of me. They all thought because I was quiet and strange that I was wild in bed. Little did they know I wasn't a freak in the sheets. I barely had any experience at all. Even if I was experienced, I wasn't down for sex with anyone ... man or woman.

Some nights, I'd fall asleep with my hand down my pants, my fingers moving over my sensitive bundle of nerves and bringing me a release that would relax my body. On those nights, my anger toward Chet would wane, and I'd imagine he was touching me.

In my imagination, he would whisper demands and make me beg. In my imagination, he would touch me where my body needed to be touched and make me come so hard I'd cry out his name in my empty apartment.

It worked.

Solitude.

Anger.

Masturbation.

My drums.

It all worked.

So when the girls wanted to get together to celebrate the completion of album number three, I was all for a party. I drove over to Lena's place, which was ten minutes from my apartment, and when I entered, the girls were already screaming with joy and celebrating loudly with hugs.

"What's going on? What's all the excitement about?"

The girls turned my way, their eyes full of joy and their smiles big.

"We're going on tour again," Twiggy said as she clapped out her happiness.

I loved touring. Not that I'd been on many tours. A small one, followed by Rock Across America, which was huge. But being on tour meant staying busy, and staying busy meant not thinking about my past. Not thinking about the things that destroyed me.

I joined the girls in their joy, already planning what I needed to pack. The last time we toured, I had forgotten some essentials that I wouldn't forget again.

"Oh, my God, this is going to be so fun." Lena giggled. "And lucky you, Constance, you get to spend the entire tour with your new hubby."

And just like that, all the happiness and excitement were sucked from the room. The walls closed in, hovering at my sides and squishing me. The air around us grew thick with anxiety, and my heart sped up with panic.

"What do you mean?" I asked, trying to mask my worry.

Lena turned my way, her eyes shining and her cheeks flushed. "We're headlining *with* Blow Hole! Oh, my God, the crowds are going to be fucking huge."

Their chatter turned to white noise, and sweat popped from my pores, covering my face in a slick sheen.

I'd barely made it through the last tour with Blow Hole. I wasn't sure I could do it again ... especially right after the last one. It had only been a few months since the previous tour. I was still coming down from the deep depression and anger I'd hoarded around for the two-month tour.

There was no getting out of it. I had to suck it up and go with the flow since it was my job. I had to think about more than just my sanity. I had to think about what was good for my family... the girls. And if that meant putting myself in the path of a hollow point bullet, then so be it.

I'd remember.

I'd explode.

I'd die.

But while I was doing all those things, I'd play the fuck out of my drums and help my girls make it to the top.

4

CHET

The Bad Intentions tour started on a Saturday in Seattle. The venue we were playing was twice the size of anything we'd played before. The crowds were large and wild, trying to climb onto the stage and fighting in the front row. Women even pulled their shirts over their heads and showed their goods.

A smoky haze covered the crowd like a sheet, making it look like we were playing among the clouds. It was appropriate, considering the crowd made us feel like stars. It was fucking amazing.

By that first night, I had a pretty brunette in the back room of the venue we were playing. She was a groupie. I'd seen her before, and because she was recognizable to me meant she followed our shows. That was fine by me. If she wanted a piece of me, she could have it.

Women liked me.

It was my gift.

It was my curse.

"Ah, fuck," I moaned.

My head rolled back on my shoulders as I received the best blowjob. Of course, every blowjob I got was the best I'd ever had. It was a fucking blowjob. Unless she used her teeth and gnawed on my junk, it was good. A mouth on my cock and balls would never be wrong.

My back pressed into the wall behind me as I pressed my fingertips against the back of her skull until she gagged. Her throat closed around me like a hug, and the pleasure in my balls spiked.

Thick saliva coated my junk and dripped from underneath as she continued to suck as if her life depended on it. She was a fucking champ.

"More," I demanded.

She sucked me deeper, taking me completely, and I hissed when she pushed her finger deeper into my ass. The sensations of her mouth on my cock and her middle finger swirling in my asshole were amazing.

She was a keeper ... if I was into keeping, which I wasn't. But it was rare to find a woman who stuck a finger in your ass and knew how to use it.

"Get ready for it, baby," I warned.

Some women didn't mind a little Chet shot in the back of their throats. Some women did. Something told me Ass Fingerer was all for it. And when she deep throated my shaft and began to hum, I knew it was go-time, and she was game.

My fingers tingled from the pressure I was putting on the back of her head as I unloaded down her throat. Like the champ I knew she was, she swallowed it all, sucking my juices from my body like an expensive wine.

When I was finished, her finger slipped from my ass and sent another jolt of pleasure down into my balls. The wall held me up as my body melted against it.

"Damn, baby," I cooed, tucking her curled hair behind her ear. "That was amazing. That was really fucking amazing."

She looked up at me with a smile before standing and swiping at the corners of her mouth.

"You taste good."

I nodded. "I know."

I noticed movement from the corner of my eye, and I turned to see Hope standing in the doorway staring back at us with her usual disgusted expression. Her eyes moved over me before landing on my deflating cock. Instantly, it sprang to life again right before her eyes.

She looked up at me and shook her head as if she was shocked.

What I was doing wasn't shocking. Everyone knew my game, and I was sure Hope knew, too.

"You want dibs on this?" I asked her, pointing down at my fresh hard-on. "I can take both of you no problem, but only if you girls show me some hot scissoring action."

I was only half-joking. I knew I couldn't fuck with Hope. I knew the consequences of fucking people who were close to your friends, but still, it was fun joking around about it. Plus, I couldn't lie; if she agreed, I'd totally watch these two go at it.

"I'm down if she is," Ass Fingerer said with a grin.

"You're disgusting, Chet," Hope spat.

I chuckled. "Oh, come on. You'll love it. You just bump your cunts together until you get off. It's sexy. I promise."

"Fuck you," she said, turning away.

Again, I snickered. "Deal. Let's do this."

I reached into my back pocket like I was searching for a condom, and when I looked back at the door, Hope was gone.

"Is she your girlfriend?" Ass Fingerer asked.

"Nope. I don't really do the girlfriend thing. Listen," I started as I tucked my cock into my jeans and zipped them, "this was fun. Thanks, babe."

"Anytime," she purred. "It was nice meeting you."

I reached out and grabbed a handful of her ass. "It was definitely nice meeting you."

She kissed me on the cheek before we parted ways just outside the room we'd used.

I didn't get her name.

I didn't need it.

I was sure I'd see her again unless she was finally satisfied she'd gotten a taste of me, but it wasn't like I'd ever fuck with her twice. I couldn't take the chance of any girls developing feelings and all that bullshit.

It was raining, of course, when I left the venue and started toward our bus. Seattle was always so fucking wet. After living in South Carolina all my life before moving to California, I was accustomed to the sun on my skin. That rarely happened in Seattle.

I missed the East Coast—the roots of the giant oaks and the mossy canopies. I missed the palms on the Isle of Palms and the Carolina coastline. I missed the sense of home that I couldn't seem to get from California—the sense of belonging even though I'd never really had a family there.

The boys didn't seem to miss it. Probably because their homes were with their families ... their wives, and kids, but I didn't have that. Therefore, home was nowhere. I wasn't even sure if I could feel that back in South Carolina, but once the Bad Intentions tour was over, I was going to go back and see.

I wasn't paying attention to my surroundings as I whistled on my way to the guys. My brain mingled with memories of my past and how things were before everything changed. Even with the heaviness on my chest, I felt relaxed. Maybe it was because I was still pumped from our show earlier. Perhaps it was because I'd just unloaded in some chick's mouth. Either way, I felt lighter.

I spotted Hope headed my way when I was almost at the bus. She was walking with a determined stride, her face turned away as if she didn't notice me in her path. She ignored me. It was what she did, but I was the kind of man who enjoyed being ignored. Even if she only threw hatred my way, I still wanted her attention.

"Did you enjoy the show?" I called out as we approached each other.

My laughter echoed in the cooling air around me.

She could take my question a few ways. Either I was asking her if she enjoyed our show earlier in the night, or I was asking if she'd enjoyed the mini porn I'd performed not fifteen minutes before in the venue.

She didn't respond.

Instead, she continued to trek in my direction, her attention glued on whatever was to her left, which was nothing.

"Left you speechless, huh?" I joked. "That happens to the best of 'em. Don't let it get you down, baby."

And then she stopped and looked at me, her dark eyes burning holes through my body like laser beams from three feet away. I'd stopped walking, too, as I waited for her response.

"I'm not your fucking baby," she spat.

Exhilaration flew through my veins. I loved a good argument, especially with a woman like Hope. I was so used to her ignoring me that even her angry words sent a jolt of joy through me.

"She speaks." I gasped in exaggeration. "I can't believe it. That's twice today."

She shook her head in aggravation.

"Don't get used to it," she said as she began to step around me.

Without thinking, I reached out and grabbed her arm, stopping her. Her skin was soft and warm beneath my fingertips, and her scent mixed with the rain was more than amazing.

She ripped her arm from my grasp and spun around on me, rainbow-colored strands stuck to her wet cheeks.

"Don't ever fucking touch me again. Got it?"

Her chest heaved with her deep, angry breaths. Her tiny fists were balled up at her sides like she was waiting to take a swing at me. The raw hatred—the heat from her wrath—was such a turn-on. It was hot. Actually, it was fucking sexy.

My cock twitched behind my zipper, lengthening as it grew.

I held my hands up in defeat and suppressed my laughter.

"Fine. I won't touch you again." I leaned in closer and breathed her in. "At least not until you ask me to."

She chuckled sarcastically. "That will *never* happen."

"Why? Because you're immune to men?" I moved closer, aware of her tiny fists. Her sweet scent and the cleansing rain moved over me. "Let me ask you something, Hope. And I'm being completely serious. Are you a lesbian?"

She gaped at me, her eyes and mouth wide.

"Because if you are, I have no problem sharing a hot plate of wet pussy with you." I smirked. "Tell me your type, and I'll find us a girl. You can call it a peace offering."

Her eyes narrowed, her teeth showing as she gritted them together.

"You disgust me."

I laughed.

The women who weren't fucking me were always disgusted by me. It was more about them than it was about me.

"I'll take that as a yes," I responded.

I'd wondered if maybe Hope was a lesbian, but then I'd see her creeping around with another dude from some other band with that just-had-sex look, and I wasn't so sure. Maybe she was like me. Maybe she swung all kinds of ways. Either way, I knew I'd gotten under her skin, which was what I'd set out to do from the moment I'd seen her walking my way.

She moved to go around me once more, and I stopped her again, pulling my hands from her arm just as quickly as I'd put it there.

I knew girls like Hope, and she wouldn't hesitate to knock the shit out of me.

"Is there a reason why you hate me so much?"

It wasn't what I meant to ask, but it came out without much thought.

For months, I'd wondered where her hatred had stemmed from. If I had done something, I honestly didn't know I'd done it. What I did know was the animosity she held against me made things uncomfortable for the guys and the girls of Red Room Sirens. They never mentioned it, but it was obvious to everyone around us that Hope had issues with me.

"Who says I hate you?"

"Stop the shit, Hope. It's obvious."

She sighed in aggravation and rolled her eyes toward the weeping sky.

"Just because I don't open my vagina hole for you every second of every day doesn't mean I hate you. Just because I don't drop to my knees and blow you like your cock is chocolate-covered gold doesn't mean I hate you. Just drop it, Chet."

Thinking of her doing all the things she'd just mentioned was the cherry on top. My cock was hard and ready. I reached down and adjusted myself through my jeans for comfort, but the outline of my cock was more than visible.

Her eyes moved over my dick, and it throbbed at her attention.

"Seriously?" she asked.

Oh, yeah. I was always serious when it came to my dick.

"What?" I asked with a shrug. "Fighting with you gets me hard, but when you go and start talking about blowing me and fucking me, it gets worse."

When she moved to go around me, she threw her shoulder into my side like a tiny football player. It was funny, so I laughed.

Turning, I watched the sway of her ass in her ripped jeans as she power-walked toward the venue. Chains hung from her pockets, clinking in the rhythm of her walk.

Sexy. As. Fuck.

I wouldn't do it because I didn't want to cause any issues within the group, but the desire to fuck Hope was growing. Her little fits of rage were a turn-on, and when I closed my eyes, I could imagine her taking that rage out on me as she power rode the fuck out of my cock.

The following day, we left Seattle and headed to our next show in Vegas, Sin City. I slept through most of the ride, but it was hard to get any fucking sleep with Tiny and Constance in the back room fucking and Zeke and Finn pining away for their wives.

I was happy for them, I really was, but that didn't mean I didn't miss the old days. I missed the days when the boys and I would fuck up the city of Vegas. We would tear the place apart, living in the VIP sections of the hottest clubs and drinking the finest of everything. I longed for the days when they were down for a good time just as much as I was.

Now, I spent most of my time feeling like an outsider. I was the adopted hindrance no one wanted—the nuisance—the one most likely to get the guys in trouble. I was an annoyance for the boys—someone who called them to pick me up when I was too fucked up to drive home or find a cab. The boys had never said as much, but I wasn't stupid. I knew who I was.

It was my life, though, and I wasn't changing my ways anytime soon.

We played two shows in Vegas, bringing the house down and throwing in a few songs that weren't on our albums. After our set, I stayed on the side stage and watched the Red Room Sirens play.

They were good.

No.

They were better than good.

Lena had a set of lungs on her that echoed throughout the venue and almost engulfed the instruments. Her long, dark hair blew in the soft breeze from the foggers and gave her an ethereal presence. She was pretty and sang with heart, but she wasn't as hardcore as some of the other girls in the group were.

Constance's guitar playing rivaled Zeke's. She was so good, in fact, that we had no problem whatsoever letting her fill Zeke's spot a while back when he had crushed his fingers.

I could see why Tiny was so in love with her. She played hard, but she loved even harder. I could see that every time she looked at Tiny—every time she put her all into what they were building together.

Mia's bass line vibrated the venue, adding that extra something to each song they played. Mia was the something spicy in the group. With her thick thighs and beautiful cleavage, she drove the guys in the crowd wild. I couldn't lie, I'd looked, but for some reason, I couldn't get into Mia. She was too much like a younger sister or something.

Twiggy played her keyboard, her thin arms flexing as she pressed her fingers on the keys like her life depended on it. We didn't have anyone on keys, but I had to admit, it added to their sound and rounded them out. Twiggy was tall and skinny, but she played like a beast.

But it was Hope who held my attention.

She was amazing on the drums—her tempo precise—her use of the drumsticks artistic. The muscles in her arms gleamed under the lights, her tattoos coming to life with each move she made. Her expression reminded me of a woman in the throes of passion—her release so extreme as it moved through her arms, into her sticks, and landed on her drum set.

She was a show on her own, and I couldn't take my eyes off her. I'd always been curious about Hope, but seeing her play—her love of the drums—made her an enigma.

I wanted to know more.

No.

I needed to know more.

I found myself staying to watch her play instead of letting a groupie climb all over me, and that in and of itself was a big fucking deal for a dude like me.

I stayed glued to the spot, and for the first time in a long while, I enjoyed watching other people play. I hadn't been to a concert in years, but when the Sirens played, they brought the house down.

"They're good," Finn said at my side.

I hadn't even realized he was standing beside me. I'd been so engrossed in Hope and how she beat the shit out of her set.

"Yeah."

"The boys and I were talking. Whatever beef you have with Hope, squash it."

I turned his way, taking in his nonchalant expression. "There's no beef ... at least, not for me."

He chuckled. "It's more than obvious to everyone. Whatever it is, try to fix it, man. It's bad for morale around here."

I nodded. "I'll see what I can do."

I turned away, putting my attention back on the girls, but I could feel Finn's gaze on the side of my face.

"I'm worried about you, Chet."

I nodded, keeping my eyes on the girls. "I know you are."

"Do I need to worry?"

He was feeling me out. I wasn't sure why Finn was starting to worry suddenly. Maybe because I was living alone for the first time since joining the band. Maybe because they'd all moved on and had families while I had no one.

He didn't need to worry, though. I'd be fine. I'd be okay until I wasn't. Of course, by then, no one could save me.

"Nope. I'm good, man."

I hated lying to Finn. He was one of my best friends, and I wasn't much for lying, but some things were better left unsaid. So I would continue to pretend everything was okay, even though it wasn't.

"I know you're lying to me, but you'll tell me when you're ready."

I nodded, and he walked away from me toward the exit. Seeing Finn after our show was rare since, usually, he'd go straight for his phone and sit on the bus talking with Faith and the kids.

That night, both bands had a night out on the town. We took over the VIP sections of every club we hit, which made it hard for me to meet any women since women weren't really allowed in anymore. That was just another change once the guys got married.

I still had a great time, though. Finn and Zeke even did some shots with us. We laughed and drank, and for a while, it felt just like old times again ... minus the women, of course.

A few hours later, my headache began. It started out as a soft ache in my temple, but before long, it split my head in two, pounding so fiercely with the music that I thought I'd be sick. Still, I drank through the pain, drowning it out entirely with hard liquor until I was too buzzed to care that my head felt as though an elephant was sitting on top of it.

"Check this out, man," Zeke said, holding his sleek smartphone my way.

The screen lit up with three females—all blond—all so ridiculously beautiful it made my heart ache. Zeke's daughters had me wrapped around their little pinky fingers. I would do anything for them. So when he showed me the picture of the three of them—all bright smiles, all blue eyes—my heart melted.

"I love those little girls." I leaned back on the couch and took a deep swig from my beer.

"They love you, too. I miss them so fucking much." He darkened his screen and stuffed his phone into his pocket. "I remember when all I could think about was the music and the tours. Now, all I can think about is going home to them. I love this job. I love playing so fucking much, man, but I love them more."

I nodded.

I understood precisely what he was saying. Even though I didn't have a family of my own, Finn and Zeke's families were like mine. Their kids treated me like their favorite uncle, and when it came to spoiling them, I was all about that shit. Their moms bitched, but I saw their secret smiles when the kids would go nuts over their new toys.

Sadness swooped over me, taking with it the tiny buzz I was enjoying. My head banged, making me flinch with the pain and reminding me that I'd never have kids. I'd never have a wife. I wasn't even sure I could settle down long enough to be faithful to one woman, but that didn't mean I didn't want the option of trying.

My eyes moved around the room, taking in the couples on the dance floor, the men and women at the bar flirting, and my group in the VIP section. Everyone around me was so happy—getting the lives they wanted—and thinking of their future.

Not me.

I had no future.

My eyes clashed with Hope's from across the VIP section, and her brows pulled down in confusion. She had been watching me, and I couldn't help but wonder what she saw.

Did she see the piece of shit I'd become?

Did she see the sickness that dwelled inside me?

Or did she see the lost little boy I felt like most days?

Sadness.

Anger.

Regrets.

I didn't know what she saw. I knew that sometimes when she looked at me, I felt like she could see more of me than anyone else could.

I was not sure I liked it very much. Being laid bare for anyone made me uncomfortable.

Looking away, I downed the shot sitting on the table in front of me. It was going to take me the rest of the night to gain my buzz back. And if I wanted to go to bed without feeling anything, including the raging headache that was busy devouring my brain, then I needed to get started right away.

5

HOPE

Something was off with Chet. He wasn't himself at all. His smiles were forced, his eyes strained. He didn't laugh as much, and he seemed to be drinking too fast—as if he were trying to drown himself. It was so glaringly obvious; I was surprised the guys didn't notice.

Maybe it was because I was getting a good look at him without women draped all over him. Maybe it was because, for the first time in a long while, he had a strange clarity in his eyes. I wasn't sure how I knew something wasn't right. I just knew.

He was sitting in the VIP section drinking with everyone, yet it was like he wasn't there. His long jeans-clad legs sprawled out in front of him, and his T-shirt was tight against his abs. His dark hair hung in his gloomy eyes as if he was trying to hide behind the inky strands, but I could see him. I'd always been able to see him.

He was somewhere else—some place far away—lost in his mind as if something was bringing him down. He was battling something, as if he was being eaten from the inside out, and I felt sorry for him.

The minute his eyes settled on mine, I felt embarrassed that he caught me staring. I'd been doing that a lot lately ... staring at Chet. I hated him for not remembering me, I really did, but I couldn't deny that I was attracted to him as well.

Every time the thought of him against me would roam into my mind, I'd curse myself. I'd shake my thoughts away each time I'd remember how good it felt to have him inside me.

He was good—the best—my only.

I looked away quickly, but his eyes remained on me. I could feel them penetrating me and learning all my dark secrets. I couldn't sit there while he figured me out. While he learned everything I was trying to hide. Instead, I stood on shaking legs and fled to the bathroom.

Twiggy followed, her small frame slipping through the massive crowd like it was nothing. Once we were inside the pink neon-covered space, I disappeared inside the closest stall and stood there trying to catch my breath.

"You okay in there, Hope?" Twiggy called out.

I could see her through the crack in the stall door. She was looking at herself in the mirror and tilting her head to the side.

Meanwhile, I was hyperventilating in a small space that smelled like piss and perfume.

I wasn't going to make it through this tour. I was slowly losing it—catching myself daydreaming about a man I could never be with, while still secretly wanting to choke the life out of him. It was beyond sick and demented, but that was me ... fucked up mentally, as always.

"Hope?" Twiggy asked again.

"I'm good. Be out in a sec," I responded.

I'd prided myself on the ability to contain my emotions, which weren't many since I squashed anything I felt the second I felt it, but I was slipping. Things were showing. My secrets were winning, and if I didn't stop myself, Chet would soon know everything. Everyone would soon know everything.

"So, what's the deal with you and Chet?"

Twiggy's words crashed into me, making me gasp. I swallowed hard and closed my eyes against the anxiety.

"I don't know what you're talking about."

41

She laughed. "Bullshit. You guys have an issue with each other. What's the story there? You guys fuck or something?"

My heart was going to beat out of my chest. I pressed the back of my head against the stall door.

Shit.

Fuck.

Damn.

"What?" I pretended to be appalled. "Hell, no. We just don't get along. No story. I just think he's gross."

Again, she chuckled. I peeked through the gap in the door to see her leaning against the countertop, waiting for me.

"I think he's hot." She giggled.

"You think everyone's hot."

"Yeah, I guess you're right. Well, you guys don't like each other. I just assumed you'd fucked, and it ended badly or something."

She was so close to the truth it was suffocating. But I didn't let on. Instead, I laughed it off.

"Hell, no … I wouldn't let that sick fuck touch me. Seriously, there's no story. I just don't like him."

"Well, squash that shit. The girls are starting to talk about it, and if we're going to be on tour with Blow Hole, we need to keep the peace."

I nodded even though she couldn't see me. "I'll see what I can do."

"Good. Are you almost done?" she asked.

"Yeah, I'll be out in a bit."

"Okay, well, I'll see you out there," she said.

The music flowed into the bathroom as she opened the door and went quiet again when the door closed behind her.

If what she was saying was true, and the girls were starting to notice that things were weird between Chet and me, then it was time I stopped making my hatred for him so obvious … even if I had to pretend to be his friend. Whatever it took, I'd do it if it meant I could get through this tour without any issues.

Thirty minutes later, I left the bathroom feeling like I could breathe. I grabbed a drink at the bar and went back to the VIP area. I spent the rest of the night in the corner downing shot after shot with the girls. The drinks went down smooth after a while, and slowly, my worries began to melt away.

The night ended earlier than usual. We were exhausted—our days full of sound checks and nights full of shows. I was never so happy to return to my quiet room, where I could snuggle in my bed and recharge. I could remove everything and lay around naked in peace and quiet. It was going to be amazing.

We split in the lobby, Constance returning to a shared room with her husband, Tiny, Lena, and Mia going out for an early breakfast, and Twiggy going for a new tattoo with Finn and Zeke.

A couple in the elevator made out as I rode the lift to the tenth floor to my room. The walls closed in on me as my buzz fizzled through my brain. I'd definitely drunk too much, but considering my circumstances, it made sense. The night had been long, and as much as I tried to stay away from Chet, I could still feel his eyes on my body—undressing me—caressing me.

When the doors opened, fresh air filled the elevator, and I took a deep breath before stepping out. My legs wobbled as I passed door after door until I was standing in front of my room. I slipped the card into the lock, and the green light flashed with a click. Pressing the knob down, I opened my door and prepared to enter when something caught my attention out of the corner of my eye.

It was Chet.

He was standing in the center of the hallway about ten doors down from me. He wasn't moving, and he was alone. His body was stiff; his hands perched on his hips. He'd been acting strange all night, but something was definitely off with him.

I closed my door and started toward him. He was facing me, yet he never looked at me. Instead, his eyes moved wildly around the hallway in confusion. Once I was close enough, I could see that sweat covered his face, and he was obviously panicking. The pulse on his tattooed neck beat furiously, making the black and red dagger inked on his skin look like it was stabbing him repeatedly.

"Chet?" I questioned softly.

He looked like he was seconds away from running away. Fear and anguish transformed his usual carefree persona into something completely different.

He didn't answer. He didn't even look at me. His eyes danced around the space we stood in as if it were an alternate reality. Instead of speaking to me, he swallowed hard and continued to hyperventilate. He was so pale—so sweaty—not his usual attractive self.

The last thing I wanted to do was touch him, but he was obviously in distress. I hated myself for the worry that worked itself into my conscience. I shouldn't care. If anything, I should be happy about his distress, considering. Instead, I reached out and laid my hand on his arm.

He was hot beneath my touch. His muscles bunched and rippled against the pads of my fingers, making them tingle. I hadn't touched Chet since that night so many years before, and all it did was remind me of being close to him. It reminded me of feeling him and becoming one with another human being. It was almost too much, but still, I wrapped my hand around his firm forearm, trying to calm him.

"Chet?" I repeated.

His eyes darted to my hand, which was resting against his tatted skin, before clashing with mine. He was dazed, without an ounce of clarity in his eyes. Whatever he'd taken, he was obviously having a bad reaction.

Drugs.

It was always something stupid like that when it came to Chet.

Fuck him for making me worry when it was the last thing in the world I wanted to do.

"What did you take, Chet?" I sighed in aggravation.

There I was, worrying that something was wrong with him when he was obviously having a bad high. I needed to figure out what he took and get him back to the boys so they could deal with him. He wasn't my responsibility.

"I didn't," he stumbled over his words.

I pushed his arm away when I lifted my hand from his skin. He was starting to annoy me. I'd had a long, stressful night, and because of him, I was losing my buzz. I wanted to go to my room and crash. The last thing I wanted was to be caught up in an empty hallway with him while he crashed from his high.

"Cut the shit, Chet. Just tell me what you took so I can take you back to the guys."

"I can't find my room," he said.

Worry flashed through his eyes, and he swallowed hard.

I shook my head, my aggravation growing.

"Well, you could start by going to the right floor. You boys aren't even staying on the tenth floor."

He blinked. "Tenth?" he asked, confused.

Again, his eyes moved from mine and over the doors around us.

"What floor are we on?" he asked.

He was fucking with me. I wasn't dumb enough to fall for his stupid shit again.

I shook my head and sighed. "I don't have time for this shit."

I turned to go back toward my room, but his hand on my arm stopped me.

My body stiffened; his touch repulsed me, yet still sent chills up my arm and more memories crashing through my brain. I tugged my arm free from his grasp and practically growled at him.

Something in his expression changed, and he went from drunk, lost, and confused to sad and fearful again.

"Please, Hope," he whispered. "Please."

My hands went to my hips, my Converse tapping quickly on the plush carpeting beneath my feet.

"What kind of game is this?" I asked, annoyed. "What are you doing, Chet?"

I didn't know this game. I wasn't sure how to play this.

"No game. Please," he begged, his expression totally opposite of anything I'd ever seen on his face. His smug, confident self was gone, and instead, there was only a frightened young boy. "Please take me to my room. I'll never ask you for anything else ever again."

I swallowed, unsure of what my next move should be. I knew the boys were on the fifteenth floor. I knew about what room Chet was staying in since I'd gone to the room Constance and Tiny were sharing and happened to see Chet come out of the room next door. But did I really want to help this man?

I'd needed him once, and he wasn't there, but it wasn't as if I'd gone to him and asked for help. It wasn't as if he knew anything. And while I'd continue to hold my sadness and regrets against him, I wasn't the kind of woman who could walk away from someone begging for help.

I nibbled my bottom lip, still unsure, but then I remembered my conversation in the bathroom with Twiggy. If I wanted to keep my secrets, I needed to make nice with Chet ... even if it was just a little nice.

I nodded.

"Come on." I turned away and started back toward the elevator.

He didn't respond, but I felt him behind me as he followed.

The button to open the elevator was warm beneath my finger, and it took forever for the lift to make it to our floor.

46

I stood there, my back straight, with Chet, my worst enemy, right behind me.

His breath shifted the hair on the back of my neck, and chills moved down my stiff spine. I scratched at the back of my neck as if to scratch the chills away.

"Thank you, Hope," he said from behind me.

His words were soft and meaningful. His words were honest, and I wanted to hate him more, but I couldn't. Something about his behavior was throwing me off my game.

"It's fine."

The doors opened as soon as the words left my mouth, and I stepped in. He followed, going to the other side of the elevator and pressing his back against the wall. Once again, we were alone.

I pushed the button for his floor and pressed my back against the wall across from him.

"You shouldn't get this fucked up, Chet," I said to fill the stagnant air surrounding us.

He didn't say anything. Instead, he nodded and turned away.

Why wasn't he saying anything?

Why wasn't he defending his actions?

Chet was the kind of guy who would.

When the elevator beeped and opened on the fifteen floor, I stepped off, and he followed. I could hear his heavy boots on the carpet with each step he took until finally, we were standing in front of his door.

The entire situation was uncomfortable for me. For months throughout the Rock Across America tour, I'd kept my distance. I'd been doing the same on this tour, but being caught alone with Chet was wrecking my nerves.

"Here you are," I said as I turned away. "I think you can take it from here."

I started back toward the elevator when again, a hand on my arm stopped me. My teeth gritted together in aggravation. I was irritated with him for touching me, but I was also annoyed with myself for liking it so much.

I looked back, my eyes landing on his, and the honesty there sickened me. His brown eyes swallowed me whole, locking me in place.

He was good. He was so fucking good at playing the lost and afraid cards. It only made me hate him more.

"Please don't tell the guys about this," he requested.

I didn't respond.

Instead, I nodded and shook his hand off my arm.

I didn't breathe again until I was in the elevator alone. And it wasn't until I was in bed and about to fall asleep that the memories of Chet came rushing over me.

Our night together many moons before.

The repercussions of that night.

And the feeling I had when I handed over my heart and left myself feeling empty and broken.

It didn't matter what Chet had gotten into. I couldn't let him get back in my head. I couldn't let myself see him as anything more than the piece of shit who crumpled me between his fingers.

I hated Chet, and when I fell asleep that night, I went to sleep with renewed purpose to stay away from him, while remaining as friendly as possible.

The girls could never know about my past, and Chet could never know the weight I carried on my shoulders every day. I'd do whatever was necessary to make sure that didn't happen.

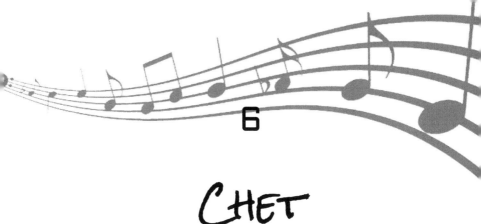

6

CHET

Since my diagnosis, I'd had some strange shit go down, but this was new. A few years back, I went blind for two days, which was the main reason I'd gone to the doctor in the first place. A few weeks after that, the migraines started. But I could say with complete surety that I'd never felt this way before.

I was lost and confused, with no clue whatsoever where I was. My heart began to beat so fast, I was afraid it was going to leap from my chest. My hands were tingling and shaking, and sweat pushed from my body in sticky waves. Dizziness swooped in, leaving me feeling unbalanced and unsure of moving.

For the first time in my life, I panicked. I hadn't even panicked that badly when I went blind, but there I was, freaking out like a scared little bitch boy.

I didn't know panic. I didn't understand how a person could be afraid of essentially nothing, but I was scared for my life. I was afraid because I was dying, which was funny considering I'd been staring death in the face every day for the past few years.

I was usually a laid-back guy. Nothing ever got to me. Mostly because of my no-care attitude, but also because fuck it, life was going to end when it was my time, but I wasn't seeing it that way at that moment. At that moment, I was grabbing on to life with greedy hands and flipping out.

I stood in the tilting hallway trying to get back to my room, and nothing looked familiar to me. The walls were closing in, and the long hallway of doors reminded me of a horror movie I'd once seen. And at that moment, the air left my lungs, and everything began to spin even faster. I struggled to breathe, grasping at the tiny bits of oxygen I could find with ravenous lungs.

I didn't know where I was, and for a few seconds, I think I forgot who I was, as well. I wasn't going to make it out of the hallway alive. I wasn't going to survive. I was dying. In the middle of a hallway in a hotel in Vegas, I was going to die.

It wasn't the drinks. It wasn't the smoke. It wasn't a bad high from our night out. Honestly, I hadn't taken anything, and while I used to drink myself stupid, I'd cut myself off an hour before leaving.

No.

This wasn't something I'd caused.

It was a symptom.

It wasn't until I saw Hope's face that reality came crashing back into me like an icy saltwater wave. I focused on her face, which was the only thing familiar to me, and I let my eyes move over her until my heart rate began to slow.

Her hair was pulled up and away from her face. Her cheeks were flushed from our night out and too many drinks. And when she looked at me, I felt her gaze everywhere—waking me up—sending me spiraling back into the now.

Heavily lined dark eyes captured mine, and the oxygen came rushing back into my lungs like a tidal wave. She was literally the only thing I could hold onto on the entire Earth at that moment. I couldn't look away from her because I was afraid if I did, I'd dissolve into nothing and die.

Her body stiffened beneath my gaze, and her teeth sunk into her bottom lip. At that moment, she was everything holding me together. Everything paused around us, and I could hear my hard breaths. The spiraling stopped, and the oxygen continued to rush into me.

I didn't take my eyes off her until she left me at my door. And once she left me, I stared at the dark wood and wondered what the fuck was happening. The room was cool when I entered. And instead of turning on a light, I crept across the room in the darkness and collapsed against the bed, feeling like I was being sucked into the mattress.

I didn't sleep that night. Instead, I lay there thinking about how lost I'd felt trying to get back to my room. I thought about how fast my heart was beating, and the absolute fear of how it felt to slowly die.

That was what was happening in the hallway. I was sure of it. But Hope had saved me, which was strange considering how much she despised me. I'd have to thank her at some point, which would suck since I couldn't admit to her what was really happening to me.

Relief came about an hour after she dropped me at my room, and I continued to feel better throughout the night. The confusion slowly melted away, leaving only the embarrassment of being seen so weak and a raging migraine.

I hated that Hope had seen me so fucked up. I'd have to talk to her and make sure she didn't tell the guys. I'd have to convince her that I'd taken something. I'd make her think I'd been drugged out of my fucking mind and drunk off my ass. Anything to take attention away from the fact that something was obviously wrong with me.

I'd gone this long without anyone finding out, so I couldn't drop the ball in the middle of a tour. I couldn't let shit fall apart right as Blow Hole was tearing up the charts and becoming a household name. I wouldn't let that happen. I'd squash any ideas she had floating around that pretty little head of hers, and I'd fill her mind with something else.

I knew what made me delusional. I knew where the confusion came from, but I didn't need anyone else to know. So I'd say and do whatever it took to make sure she believed me. I could hardly wait until the sun came up and I could go to her and fix things.

The following day, I climbed from bed after staring at the ceiling all night. I took a hot shower and got dressed. I hated confronting Hope since I knew she despised me for whatever crazy reason she had planted in her mind, but I needed to get to her before she met up with the girls and told them everything.

Constance would know something wasn't right, and she'd go to Tiny. It would be a domino effect from that point on until Zeke, Finn, and Tiny were all breathing down my back looking for answers I wasn't ready to give. It was the last thing I wanted. It was the last thing the band needed.

I took the elevator down to the tenth floor. I wasn't sure what room she was in, but I'd knock on every fucking door on the floor if I had to. Luckily, I didn't have to do that. Once I took three steps down the long hallway of doors, she stepped out of her room as if I'd conjured her.

Shutting the door behind her, she turned my way and went still.

"Can we talk?" I asked, knowing she would probably turn me down.

She stood there, stuck beneath my gaze, as I took in her thin T-shirt, which showed her dark bra underneath, and her tight jeans. Her hair was down and wet from her shower, making the rainbow colors in her hair muted and darker.

Her elfin face was clear of all makeup, making her look younger and somewhat familiar, which made no sense. Of course, she looked familiar. I'd seen her often over the last three months.

She reached up and pushed her wet hair from her clean face. I loved that about Hope. She could dress up, lining her dark eyes and adding color to her lips, or she could dress down in her jeans and T-shirts and put her hair in knotted updos. But at the same time, she didn't give a fuck about what she looked like, and something about that made her sexy as hell.

She nodded and stuck the card key into her door to open it again. Once the door was open, she went inside, and I followed her in.

Her room was clean, her clothes organized and tucked away. It wasn't what I imagined Hope's room to look like. She was so rock 'n' roll, so fucking crazy. I pictured a room that looked as if a hurricane had hit it. I imagined the maid services cursing her as they cleaned her room daily.

It looked as if the maid service had already come through. Her bed was made, the sheets and covers tucked perfectly, but I knew it was still too early for that.

She set her card key on the table by the door and stepped farther into the room. Picking at her chipped black nail polish, she stood, nibbling her bottom lip.

"What do you want, Chet?"

She was annoyed.

I didn't blame her.

I was annoyed with myself, too.

"I want to talk about last night." The words were sticky on my tongue.

She shrugged. "There's nothing to talk about."

Not true.

We had a ton to talk about, and she wasn't leaving until I was sure she would keep what happened between us.

She moved toward the door again as if our conversation was over.

It wasn't.

"I fucked up last night." I chuckled, trying to cover my anxiety. "I mixed some pills with my drinks. Anyway, I just wanted to apologize for fucking with you last night," I lied.

I hadn't mixed anything with anything, but she didn't need to know that.

She didn't respond.

Instead, she stood there with her arms crossed, staring me down. I could tell by her expression that she could sense I was lying. I wasn't very good at telling lies since I never did. I didn't need to. I was blunt and usually didn't give a fuck, but this time was different. I needed her to believe it was drugs and not anything else.

Finally, she nodded and looked away. She stared at the curtained windows of her room, the sun sending yellow beams of light into her tidy room.

"I've never seen you act like that," she stated.

She'd never paid any attention to me, so I wasn't sure what that meant. On occasion, I'd catch her staring at me, but that was rare, and usually when she was drunk. As far as I knew, I was the last person on Earth she wanted to give an ounce of attention to.

"I'm sure you've never seen me act a lot of ways."

She shook her head. "No. I've been on tour with you twice now. I've seen you do stupid shit. I've watched you with a different woman every day. I've seen you so drunk you couldn't stand—so high you couldn't stop smiling—but I've never seen you lost and confused. I've never seen you afraid."

Fuck.

This wasn't good.

I had to figure out a way to fix this. I had to think of a way to make my 'too many drugs and drink' story stick. Either that or I had to take her mind off it completely, and there was only one sure way I could do that.

"So you watch me, huh?" I smirked, changing the subject to something I was comfortable with.

Flirting and sex.

She turned away from the windows, and her eyes landed on mine. They were wide, as if she'd been caught doing something she wasn't supposed to do.

"That's not what I'm saying," she said quickly.

She crossed her arms once again, her arms pushing her tits up higher as if she were serving them up for me.

I moved. Being closer to her was suddenly something I desired. I wanted to smell her freshly shampooed hair and feel her soft skin beneath my fingers. I wanted to taste her. All things I couldn't really do, but all things I knew would send her mind reeling in the opposite direction of last night's situation.

She backed away with each step I took in her direction, and I grinned when I saw her throat tighten with her nervous swallow.

"That's what it sounded like to me." I moved closer, my knee brushing hers. "It sounds like you can't keep your eyes off me."

Her breathing accelerated, her chest rising and falling quickly. I was getting to her. I'd never thought it was possible with how obviously she hated me, but I was definitely getting to her.

"You're pissing me off," she threatened, her hand going to my chest as she pushed me away. "Stop, Chet."

"Stop what? Stating the truth?"

Her eyes narrowed, and her lips pinched in anger.

"This is bullshit." She sighed.

I wasn't expecting that reaction.

"What's bullshit?"

She pushed at my chest again, and this time, I moved away from her.

"Twiggy says I should try to be your friend. She says it would be better for the tour if I could get along with you."

Her words sounded familiar. I'd gotten the same speech from Finn.

"But I can't be your friend if you're pushing up on me and shit. I'm never going to fuck you. Never. If you can accept that, then maybe we can get along well enough to get through this fucking tour. But if not, I can promise I will put my fist through your face."

Well, fuck.

That was about as blunt as it got.

My respect for her moved up several notches, and I felt myself backing away even farther from her.

I nodded my understanding. "I can accept that. But if we're going to be friends, I need something other than sex from you."

Again, her eyes narrowed, and her shoulders stiffened. I'm sure she was expecting something sexual.

"And what would that be?" she asked.

"I need you to promise you'll never mention last night to anyone ... ever."

Her shocked eyes moved over my face. She hadn't expected that.

"If you can promise me that, we can be best friends for fucking life as far as everyone else is concerned."

I waited and watched as she thought it over, and finally, she nodded and uncrossed her arms.

"I promise, but you shouldn't let yourself get that way, Chet. We're here to work. Keep your shit together, man."

I chuckled and nodded. "I will."

At least, I would try to keep my shit together. It wasn't like I had much control over the situation. It wasn't like I could make the symptoms disappear or stop entirely.

I'd have to find a way to make sure it never happened again in front of anyone. Or worse, that it never happened on stage during a show. I don't know what I'd do if I suddenly forgot how to play or couldn't remember the beats for each song. That would suck so much ass.

I held my hand out. "So, friends?"

Her eyes went to my hand as if it was a snake, but slowly, she reached out and shook it. "Friends."

I left her room feeling as if I'd accomplished something. I'd secured her promise that she wouldn't tell anyone about the night before, and I trusted that she wouldn't. But I'd also squashed whatever issues Hope had with me. The tour would be a smooth ride from that moment on ... at least as long as I could keep my brain from screwing me over.

HOPE

F riends.

I was now *friends* with Chet Rhodes.

I wasn't sure how long it would work, but if it meant taking the attention away from me and any connection with him, I'd do it. The tour wouldn't last forever, and soon, I would be away from him and everything he stood for. I could move on, focus on work, and get my life together.

Our next stop was in Phoenix, and when I stepped off the bus and into the dry heat, I was sent back to a time when I enjoyed the hot summers of South Carolina. I'd spend the day outdoors away from my parents, and I wouldn't go home until I was sure they had both passed out and would leave me alone.

My back ached when I stretched in the sunlight. Sleeping on a bunk was really starting to get annoying. It made me long for the stops when we parked for more than a day and would stay in a booked room. I didn't really sleep well in the bunks, but on a king bed in a five-star hotel, I could sleep like a queen.

"Fuck, it's hot out here," Mia said as she stepped off the bus. "The boob sweat is legit."

She was wearing large black shades that covered the majority of her face. She'd piled her hair on top of her head in a messy bun, and she was still wearing her pajamas. We all were. Except mine were *Star Wars* and boyish, and hers were purple and cute.

"Holy shit! Who turned up the heat?" Lena followed. "The crack of my ass is starting to sweat."

I laughed.

It was hot, but it was also nice.

We spent a good chunk of the day doing our sound check and then left the venue for an early dinner before the show. Both bands and a few crew members took up the entire VIP section at one of Phoenix's hottest restaurants, and we ate and had a few drinks.

"When we get to New Orleans, I'm hitting Bourbon Street so hard. I've never been there," Lena said.

Chet laughed, making us all turn his way. "Don't get too excited. Bourbon Street smells like hot shitty ass."

"Shut up. No, it doesn't," I countered.

He nodded his head. "It does. It stinks so bad they clean the streets every morning with lemon juice."

"He's right." Zeke chuckled. "Holy shit, did I just say that Chet was right?"

The guys started laughing, and I couldn't help myself; I laughed, too.

It felt strange. For the first time in a long while, I felt lighter. Like becoming friends with Chet and letting all the bullshit go for a bit had lightened my heart. I laughed with the girls and joked with the guys, and I had a great time doing it.

The waitress cleared away our dinner dishes, and I didn't miss how she smiled down at Chet when she took his plate. He leaned to the side to look at her ass when she walked away from our table.

"I'd like to tongue punch her fart box," Chet whispered to Zeke.

I know the rest of us weren't supposed to hear it, but I had.

"Dude, could you not talk about eating ass while we're eating?" Mia blurted.

59

I nodded in agreement.

"What? Ass is good for you." He grinned my way. "A piece of ass a day keeps the blue balls away."

"Oh, shut the fuck up! There's no such thing as blue balls, and you know it," Twiggy interrupted.

Every guy at the table turned to her with wide eyes.

"No comment," Finn muttered, making the guys at the table burst into laughter.

The rest of the dinner flowed in the same manner, and it wasn't long until we were in a black SUV headed back to the venue to play our set.

"Looks like things are friendlier with you and Chet," Twiggy pointed out.

"Yeah, I noticed that, too," Lena agreed. "Did you guys finally squash your issues?"

"Guys, there were no issues. We just weren't very talkative, is all," I lied.

"What changed since Vegas?" Twiggy asked.

"Nothing changed. We just haven't had many opportunities to talk. We did tonight. It's no big deal ... seriously."

Thankfully, they quit talking about it, and the conversation turned to the show tonight. We were making a slight change in the song lineup, but with us going on after the main show, we had plenty of time to get our shit together.

We went on after Blow Hole. Not because we were the more popular band because we weren't. We went second because the boys had asked us to. Mostly because Finn and Zeke wanted to be back on the bus so they could Facetime with their families before the kids were settled into bed.

It was sweet.

Lena, Mia, and Twiggy hung out on the bus while the boys played, but Constance and I sat on the side stage and watched the show. At one point during the show, Tiny turned toward Constance and mouthed the song he'd written for her.

"I'm so in love with that man," she said, her eyes still on the big beast playing the bass guitar.

"I can see that."

"I'm going to tell him when the tour is over."

"Tell him what?" I asked.

She turned my way with watery eyes and a magnificent glow I hadn't noticed before.

"I'm pregnant."

A gasp slipped from my lips, and I clutched my chest.

"Oh, my God! When did you find out?"

"Two days ago. I wasn't feeling well, and my period was late. I took a test, and sure enough." She smiled. "I'm so happy about it."

"Congratulations, babe." I leaned over and hugged her. "You're going to be a kickass mom."

At that, she chuckled sarcastically. "Poor kid."

"No, lucky kid ... he or she will have two rock star parents. The minute the baby is born, it'll be a celebrity."

At that, Constance's face dropped. "My dad was a rock legend. I'll never let this baby live the life I lived."

And then she walked away, leaving me to remember all the bullshit she'd gone through just a few months before. I was fucking famous for putting my foot in my mouth, and I'd done it again. I brought up the past she wanted to forget, and I understood that better than anyone else.

I'd have to apologize to Constance the minute we were alone again, and I needed to remember that just because she was raised differently from me, with the money and status, didn't mean she'd had a better life. We all had our demons. That included Constance and her legendary rock star daddy.

We played our set, and out of the corner of my eye, I saw Chet watching us play from the side stage. I always played better when I knew the guys were watching, and this show was no different. I played so hard and fast that the sweat was dripping into my eyes.

I downed five water bottles, hydrating myself and even dumping some over my head to combat the Arizona heat. My sleeveless Misfits tee stuck to my skin, pulling at my arms when I tried to lift them, prompting me to pull it over my head and toss it to the side.

The crowd lit up with my little strip show, and the girls laughed, their voices echoing throughout the venue through their mics. I played even better in just my black sports bra and decided that I might continue to play half-naked the way Chet did.

After the show, we said our goodbyes to Phoenix and left the stage at a run for our bus. The crew members surrounded us once we broke through the exit door, where hundreds of waiting fans welcomed us.

I stayed in the back, letting the girls lead the way. I'd wrapped my soaked tee around my neck, and I wrung out the ends as I jogged behind my group. The crowd was a bit wilder than usual, and some of the crew guys had to be a little more forceful, but I kept moving, ready to get on the bus, shower, and climb into my bunk.

Then it happened.

The crowd came together in front of me, blocking me from the rest of the group as they jogged to the bus. A wall of drunk and rowdy fans trapped me, taking pictures and asking questions.

I stopped jogging and backed away, bumping into another wall of fans. They were closing in on me; forming a circle around me and making me feel like a trapped animal.

"Let me through, guys. I need to catch my bus," I yelled out above the crowd's rumble.

I tried to remain calm and seem unbothered by my situation, but I couldn't see any of the crew members because many of the people closing in the circle were much bigger than I was. I would be ripped to shreds if the girls and the crew didn't notice I was missing and come back for me.

A man stepped into the circle, throwing his arm around me and pulling me into his large body.

"Holy shit, Nate! I'm with the drummer. Take a picture of us together. Hurry up!" he slurred.

His meaty hand moved down my back and grabbed my ass cheek.

I shook him loose and pushed him away. "What the fuck, dude? Not cool. Keep your hands off the goods."

"Ah, come on, baby. I have a ticket. I paid for a tiny touch."

He moved close again, and again, he pulled me to his body. I shoved him away and balled up my fist, ready to strike.

"I'm not fucking around, man. Touch me again, and I'll fuck you up."

The big fucker dared to laugh at me before moving again; trying to pull me by the tee I had around my neck. When I pulled back, he tugged harder on the tee, jerking my neck forward until I slammed against his hard chest.

I pushed back and swung for his face, but before my fist could make contact, a hand came out of nowhere and caught my fist.

"Whoa," Chet muttered at my side. "Easy, Short Stack. If you poke the bear, he might bite you," he whispered my way.

Then he turned toward the guy pulling on me and getting too rough and shook his shoulder as if they were longtime friends.

"What's up, bro? Everything good here?"

He was calm. Obviously, he'd been dealing with drunken, crazed fans longer than I had.

The man's face lit up when he realized Chet was talking to him.

"Holy fuck, Nate! Get a picture, man." He pulled me to his other side as if he were trying to get a picture with both Chet and me, and I gave in and smiled so his friend Nate could snap a photo.

But when I started to walk away, he pulled me back again.

"Come on, babe, don't you want to party with my boy and me."

I didn't get a chance to respond.

Chet moved between the crazy fan and me. He was just as tall as the drunk was but not as large.

"For real, man, chill out with that shit. The ladies don't like to be grabbed."

The big guy laughed loudly and pushed into Chet's space as if he was ready to start something.

"And if I don't."

The crowd around us was getting louder and closing in, making me feel like I couldn't breathe.

Pulling on Chet's arm, I got his attention. He looked down at me with a question in his eyes.

"Let's just go," I muttered.

But he wasn't hearing it. He was already amped up. I could see it in the slamming pulse on the side of his neck and the reddened glare he was throwing the big man's way.

"If you touch her again, I'll break your fucking fingers."

I gasped, shocked that Chet, the man I wasn't fond of, was taking up for me.

In that minute, something shifted. I couldn't muster up any of the hate I'd carried around for him, but instead, I felt a tiny bit of respect seep into my core.

Luckily, no punches were thrown, and no asses were kicked. The crew decided at that moment to break up the crowd around us and get us to the safety of our buses.

We were pulled apart, him taken to the Blow Hole bus, and me returned to the Siren's bus. Because of that, I didn't have a chance to thank him for helping me out.

I'd be sure to thank him the minute I could, but until then, I'd spend the drive to Houston wondering when Chet had turned into a decent guy. Because by stepping in and helping me out, he'd become just that, in my opinion.

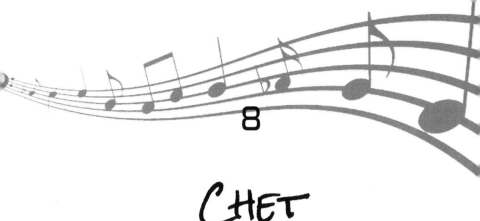

8

CHET

The drive to Houston from Phoenix took forever. I slept through most of it while the guys played video games and talked to their wives. I could hear their conversations from where I was laying, and again, I longed for someone to call home to.

I lay in my bunk and battled a migraine while secretly fantasizing of Hope in just her black sports bra, soaking wet and playing the drums. I'd never seen anything so sexy in my entire life. Sure, we were supposed to be friends, but that didn't mean I couldn't get hard thinking of the hotness of watching her play my favorite instrument half-naked.

I'd watched her as she played. Her body was wet and sweaty, her muscles flexing with each hit of her drumsticks, making me want to step on the stage and touch her. I'd watched her play many times while we toured with the Sirens, but she'd never stripped in a hot, wet rush.

Fuck!

It was sexy.

I was worked up and ready to get on the bus and crash, but I stayed behind with the intention of watching her walk away. Because of that, I got a front-row show to the assholes who stopped her and basically attacked her.

By the time we got out of the scuffle and the crew had ushered me to my bus, I was ready to put my fist through someone's face. I didn't usually get so worked up. I was the kind of person who would rather shake your hand than fight you, but the minute I saw him put his hands on Hope's soft skin and tug at her, I was done.

I wasn't sure what that meant. It was probably just my protective streak rearing its ugly head because I would have done the same for any of the Sirens. I considered them my friends. Hell, Constance was more like a sister now that she married Tiny. But it felt like more than just my protective streak. Something about the way he was touching her made me a bit jealous.

Jealousy didn't make any sense to me. Hope wasn't mine—she would never be mine, and I would never be hers. I wasn't that kind of dude, but I couldn't deny it. It was there, lingering just below the surface and mixing with my anger.

I had to shake that shit off. Jealousy didn't look good on anyone, and I was determined that no woman would ever get me fucked up. I had too much on my mind to let that shit happen, including the elephant that had taken up residence in my brain, making it split and throb.

Houston was just as hot as Phoenix, but thankfully, the venue we were playing in was nice and cool. We had two shows in Houston, which meant we got rooms for the night. I'd never been more thankful for a long, hot shower and a king-size bed.

Our first show wasn't until the following day, so we went to our rooms first thing. My shower was long and hot, and then I crashed for another hour to ease my migraine a bit. It wasn't happening, though. No matter what I did, the hammer inside my brain continuously beat.

Two hours later, the guys showed up at my door, ready to head out for lunch. I threw on some clothes and went with them even though eating was the last thing in the world

I wanted to do. The SUV that drove us to the restaurant seemed to hit every bump in the road, and behind my shades, I flinched at the pain moving through my head.

I couldn't keep this up. There was no way. I'd go fucking insane if I didn't get some form of relief soon.

Everything stopped because of the now constant migraines.

The women.

The drugs.

Everything.

All I could think about was the pain in my head and why that pain was there. I wasn't beating this, and soon, I'd lose completely.

Stepping away from the group, I pulled out my cell and made a phone call to my doctor, Doctor Patel, back in California. He'd have to call something in for the pain. I couldn't take it anymore. Maybe I was a big bitch, but the pain was breaking me down.

They didn't usually call in narcotics, but Doctor Patel was familiar with my case and knew my circumstances. He called one of his colleagues in Houston, and, long story short, I had a prescription for pain medication waiting at the local doctor's office for me.

As soon as I could, I would go there, pick up the script, and have it filled. Then I'd go back to my room, take a double dose, and sleep until the next show.

I could hardly wait for the relief.

The girls joined us at the restaurant, and thankfully, by the time my food got to the table, the migraine had let up a bit. Not entirely, but just enough that looking at my food didn't make me feel like throwing up.

Afterward, everyone wanted to grab a few drinks at the bar. Go figure, the one night I wasn't feeling it, everyone else wanted to party. I didn't bitch. Instead, I promised to meet them at the bar, took a cab to the pharmacy, and as soon as I got to the bar, I washed a pill down with my beer. If I was going to be out a while, I couldn't wait until I got back to my room.

My migraine let up a bit more, and I found myself laughing with the guys.

"Damn, Chet, when's the last time you got laid, bro?" Tiny asked.

"I think this might be a record," Zeke said.

I chuckled around the mouth of my beer. "Why are you so worried about my cock? Don't be jealous because y'all are married and not getting any."

Finn laughed. "Trust me. I get plenty."

"I know that's right," Zeke said, holding up his beer.

Tiny tapped his beer against Zeke's, making Constance chuckle and smack his arm.

"Seriously, though, what's the deal? Is your dick broken?" Finn said.

If they only knew the real reason I'd stop playing. If they only knew the real reason I'd slowed down my party lifestyle.

I hadn't touched a woman since Ass Fingerer in Seattle, and I was okay with that. I had more important shit to think about, which meant I hadn't really been looking for any playmates.

How could I perform decently when I felt like my brain was being ripped out?

"Can we not talk about my dick in front of the ladies?" I asked, nodding toward the Sirens who were snickering behind their hands.

My eyes landed on Hope, and she was the only one who wasn't smiling or laughing. Instead, she was looking at me in confusion. The way she looked at me made me feel like she knew everything I was hiding. I didn't like it.

Three beers in, and I switched to soda. I felt like a pansy-ass sipping my soda while the boys took shots, but fuck it. I needed relief in the form of a double dose of pain meds, and I couldn't do that if I drank too much. I knew I was dying. I didn't want to rush the reaper.

Hope stood and moved across the space to sit beside me. I stiffened.

Usually, she did everything she could to stay away from me, but I guess since we'd called a truce on our imaginary issues, she felt more comfortable around me.

"I wanted to thank you for the other day. It was decent of you to help me out with those dudes."

I nodded and took another drink of my soda.

"It's no biggie. The fans get crazy like that sometimes. They were just a bunch of dumbasses getting excited over a hot girl."

The second the words left my mouth, I felt uncomfortable. Flirting was normal for me, but that had been an honest moment without regard to a reward.

Her eyes went wide, and she nervously tucked a stray hair behind her ear.

"You're drinking soda." She pointed out the obvious, quickly changing the subject.

I lifted my cup and took a sip. "I am."

"Why?"

"I don't like to drink too much when we have a show coming up," I lied.

"Liar. You used to drink while you played. Sometimes you still do."

I looked at her, taking in her lined eyes and pouty lips.

How could she know what I used to do?

"I used to?" I questioned.

"Yeah, I mean, like, on the Rock Across America tour," she stumbled over her words.

"Yeah, well, things change. Maybe I want to play better, and drinking slows my arms down," I joked.

"Yeah, well, I guess if you want to play better than I do, then you should stop drinking altogether." She grinned my way.

She was being playful.

Her attitude was different.

It was new.

I kind of liked it.

"Are you saying you play better than I do?"

She chuckled before downing the shot that was sitting in front of her.

"Yeah. That's what I'm saying."

I laughed.

Not because I didn't think she was good. I knew she could play. I laughed because I was having so much fun with her, and we weren't fucking. It was new to spend time with a woman and not expect the night to end with my cock in her.

I liked it.

I liked her.

I swallowed the rest of my soda in one swig and tossed a fifty on the table.

"Come on," I said, standing from our table.

"Where are we going?" she asked.

"You think you're so much better than I am. We're going to the venue. No one's there. I say we battle it out."

She laughed, the sound loud and endearing, before she downed her last shot and stood.

"Fine. Let's go."

We took a cab back to the venue and left the rest of our bandmates back at the bar. The ride was quiet, and the tension in the air was thick. Once we were dropped off, we made our way inside. The rocks of the parking lot popped beneath her boots as I followed her. I couldn't help myself; I kept my eyes on her ass and its sway the entire way to the stage.

"Are you ready to get your ass kicked?" she asked over her shoulder with a grin.

She pulled her shirt over her head, revealing a black tank, and I had to swallow past the desire that rushed through me. She looked so fucking hot in only her boots, jeans, and a tiny tank. She obviously wasn't wearing a bra, but with tits like hers, she didn't have to.

My mind returned to the moment she was on stage in only her black sports bra. She was soaked. She was sexy. And for the first time in a couple of days, my cock grew hard.

"Let's see what you got."

I stood to the side as she sat behind my set. I didn't usually let anyone play my drums, but I trusted Hope with my babies. I'd watched her play. I knew she knew what she was doing, and I also knew she respected her own set and would do the same with mine.

She spun the sticks between her fingers, her glassy eyes all over me as she lifted a brow in challenge.

And then she brought the sticks down and beat out a fresh rhythm I'd never heard before. It was fast-paced and robust; the percussion shook the stage as she went crazy, hitting any spot on my set yet still making it sound amazing.

Her head fell back, and she closed her eyes as she continued to play, beating the drums unmercifully and turning me on beyond belief. Her arms moved, the small feminine muscles popping out with her movements, making the tattoos on her arms come to life.

I couldn't do this with Hope. I couldn't let myself get into her. She turned me on more than any woman had in years, not since my Blackbird five years earlier.

Women were a dime a dozen in my job. They were waiting just outside the venue, ready and willing to let me fuck them senseless, but I was moving past that bullshit. After everything I'd been through since we started the tour, I needed relief. But I didn't want it from just anyone.

The more I watched Hope play my drums, her arms flying and her eyes closed in ecstasy—the realization came crashing over me.

I wanted Hope.

I wanted Hope the way I'd wanted Blackbird for the last five years.

Watching her only intensified my craving for her.

I wasn't sure I could control myself. I was feeling better, my painkiller finally doing its job, and my head wasn't being ripped apart. I could think about more than the pain for once. I could think about Hope and how amazing she'd feel wrapped around me.

Wet.

Hot.

Ready.

Moving from my spot, I moved toward her. Her rhythm moved through me, vibrating my core and making me feel even more alive. I didn't stop until I was standing right beside her. She kept her eyes closed, playing with so much beauty it was breathtaking.

I reached out and took a strand of her hair between my fingers, and the colors blended together when I rubbed my fingers together. Her playing came to an instant halt, and I smirked down at her when her eyes popped open, and one of her sticks fell to the ground at my feet.

Sweat dotted the top of her lip, and her cheeks were flushed with pleasure. Her expression was one of happiness and release, and I knew playing did that for her. It did the same for me, but I wanted to give her that look. I wanted to do it with my hands and mouth ... my cock.

I moved closer, taking her cheeks in my palms and spending a minute looking at her. I didn't want it to be like the last time I felt this way. Unlike with my Blackbird, I took the time to remember everything about Hope.

I wanted to look at her face. I wanted to look into her eyes and see her when she came apart. It was going to be amazing. She was going to be amazing. We were going to be a match sexually. But before anything could go down between us, we would have to talk about it. I wanted to make sure she understood it would be a one-time thing.

Before I moved in, I wanted to ensure that this wouldn't affect the tour.

"What are you doing?" she asked.

I didn't miss the catch in her voice.

"I don't know."

And I didn't. I didn't know where this was going or what I was doing. My body was taking control of the situation, and I let it happen.

I wasn't much for kissing. I'd probably kissed a handful of women in my time, but Hope's pouty lips called to me. She was begging me to kiss her without even opening her mouth.

I leaned down, ready to taste her, but she placed her palm against my chest and stopped me.

"Wait," she whispered.

I shook my head. "No, I suck at waiting."

So I kissed her.

Hard.

She tasted like the night—liquor and sweetness with a touch of sin. It was wrong to taste her, but I'd never been one to follow the rules. All the boundaries I'd outlined regarding Hope were being crossed, but when she began to kiss me back, her tongue moving against mine, I didn't give a fuck about any limitations.

Her mouth opened, and I sucked her tongue into my mouth. Her moan vibrated through me and shot straight to my groin.

I felt her pull back, so I pressed for more, capturing her head in my hands and kissing her so deeply that I was losing myself.

My head wasn't pounding anymore, but my heart was. It was beating so hard I could hear it in my ears. My blood moved through my body like a freight train, the horns whistling loudly in my ears. I hadn't felt this kind of excitement for a woman in years, not since my Blackbird.

I couldn't stop.

I wanted more.

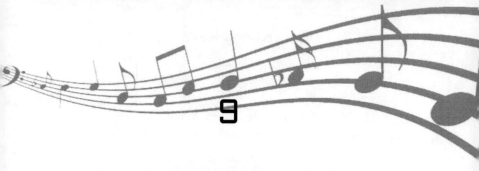

9

HOPE

He was kissing me, and I wasn't stopping him.

Why wasn't I stopping him?

His fingers melted against my skin, and his lips consumed mine so sweetly that it shocked me. Chet was rough and rowdy ... crude in a way that was usually a turn-off. I had no idea he could still be as gentle as he had been five years before.

How was Chet capable of doing this?

How could he turn it off and on so easily? Become two different men within seconds.

If I hadn't seen it with my own two eyes, I would have never believed it was possible, but everything he was doing was working, and the more he did everything he was doing, the more I leaned into him for more.

For five years, I'd sworn off men. I hadn't touched a man since that night with him. Yet there I was, letting him kiss me and enjoying it so much that I kissed him back. He tasted familiar and strangely like home. His fingers shifted into my hair, and chills spread down my back.

Somehow, he had managed to take control, and I loved every second of it. I had taken out my white flag, and I was ready to start waving it. Giving in wasn't embarrassing as long as he continued what he was doing.

I was lonely ... my body melting with needs I couldn't fulfill with my fingers and the hard, cold plastic of a vibrator. I was sick of touching myself. I wanted to feel someone else's hands on me. I needed someone to take my control away and give me a night of pleasure.

So I let go.

I pulled out my flag and waved it, moaning into him with so much relief for my decision. Our kiss was unbroken as I stood and put my arms around his neck. His tall, lean body pressed into mine, and my nipples hardened. As if he knew it felt good against my breasts, he pressed his chest against mine, and I moaned into his mouth with pleasure.

And then his lips were gone from mine, and he was pressing them against the side of my neck.

"Hope," he whispered against my skin, making my knees wobble.

My fingers went into his hair, skimming over the stubble of the shaved sides and getting stuck in the dark locks at the top. I pulled his head back and brought his lips back to mine, tasting him and losing myself in him so completely that I almost didn't hear the girls' laughter headed our way.

Then a door just off the stage slammed, and we broke apart quickly like two teenagers about to be busted. I swiped at my lips and moved away from him as Lena and the girls broke through the side stage.

Then reality came crashing back over me like freezing rain and hail, stinging my skin.

I'd given in to Chet Rhodes.

After everything I'd given him. After everything I'd lost.

I'd given in, and I'd kissed him.

I forgot all about the past and everything I lost when his lips were against mine. The darkest moments of my life, the moments that shaped me into the cold, emotionless woman, were all but swept away. I forgot about the reasons I'd left him in the middle of the night all those years ago.

How dumb could I be to make the same mistakes all over again?

Hadn't I learned my lesson?

Consequences.

Consequences.

Consequences.

I couldn't do this with Chet because I knew if I did, I'd fall for him completely like I had all those years ago. And falling for Chet wasn't safe since he wasn't the kind of man who would catch you. I'd end up splattered on the floor in pieces, except this time, I wouldn't have anything to force me to hold myself together.

If I wanted to survive, I needed to stay away from him.

End of story.

I stayed away from the side stage when the boys played. Instead, I stayed in the back room, where the girls got ready for the show. I didn't want to see him. I didn't want to even think about him, but there wasn't much I could do to make that stop.

After leaving him onstage with a raging hard-on, I returned to my room. I lay in bed with my entire body throbbing for relief until finally giving in and letting my fingers shift over the most sensitive parts of my body. Behind my lids, Chet whispered sweet words, his body making me repeatedly come until finally, everything on my body was too sensitive to touch.

Staring at my reflection as I lined my eyes and darkened my lids, the mirror in front of me vibrated with the sounds of Blow Hole and Chet's beating drums. The beat of him ticking against my skin at all times. I couldn't escape him. He was everywhere.

When it was time to hit the stage, I followed the girls out of the room. Blow Hole passed us, their energy a force to be reckoned with, but I kept my head down and away from where I knew Chet would be.

He was staring at me. I could feel his eyes as if they were touching my skin with a single fingertip. Still, I stared ahead until I was stepping up on the deck and settling behind my drum set. My palms were sweating as I gripped my sticks with white knuckles.

Lena started the show, talking to the crowd and getting them rowdy. Then I came in with the bass drum, beating out the steady thrum of the beginning of our introductory song. My arms burned when I held them above my head and beat my sticks together with the beat, and when I brought them down on the snare, my tingling fingers burned.

I played hard, blocking out the events with Chet the night before, blocking out the past completely. I beat my drums with determination, releasing my anger and hurt onto the set. The cymbals clanged louder than usual. The bass drum vibrated harder, and I knew I was going hard against everything breaking me apart.

He was there, just off the side of the stage, and his eyes were all over me, pushing me to hit harder and forcing me to keep my eyes on the crowd. I wasn't playing with the fans. I wasn't active with the girls like usual. There was just me and my drums, and that was how I played the entire set.

When the show was over, and we were being rushed from the venue to the SUVs that would take us back to our hotel, I looked to the side briefly, and my eyes clashed with Chet's. His brows pulled down in anger before I quickly diverted my attention to the girls in front of me and pretended I didn't see him.

I didn't breathe again until I was back in my hotel room and standing under the hot flow of the shower. The water stung my skin, and the heat fogged up the bathroom, making it impossible to see outside the glass shower door.

I brushed my wet hair and dressed quickly in a T-shirt and jeans, knowing the girls would come soon, and we would go out and grab some after-show drinks and food. I sat and watched TV until I heard a knock. Clicking the off button, the TV went black as I made my way to the door, ready to leave with the girls.

But when I pulled the door open, the girls weren't waiting for me on the other side. It was Chet.

10

CHET

The girls of **Red Room Sirens** had fucked up timing.

Not that I was close to fucking Hope or anything when they walked in, and we broke our kiss, but she felt so good against me, and I wasn't ready to let her go. I didn't have much choice when the girls came bursting onto the stage, making Hope pull away from me as if I was a bomb ready to explode.

Explode.

Yes.

I was so fucking ready to explode.

My cock was rock hard, throbbing harder than my recent migraines and making me want to yell for them to get the fuck out. But I knew that would never fly with Hope. She wouldn't want the girls to know about our little kiss and anything that came from it. Hell, I didn't want them to know either. It could be our little secret.

I left the girls on the stage together and returned to my room. It was the last thing I wanted to do, but it was obvious the girls weren't leaving anytime soon.

I ended up in my king-size bed with *The Big Bang Theory* on the TV and three more pain pills swimming in my stomach. I fell asleep an hour later with no pain and a smile.

• • • ● • ● ● • • •

The next day, I played better than I had in weeks. There was no headache, and I could focus on the beats and the crowd. I stripped my clothes from my body and ended up in just my boxers. The heat from playing so hard under the stage lights would make you do that. Plus, I just liked being naked. It felt good.

Hope wasn't on the side stage like usual, and for some reason, that angered me. I wanted her eyes all over me. I played better—harder—when I knew she was watching.

Why wasn't she there?

I felt like a wild man, beating my drums so hard, and sometimes standing and moving around the front of my set just because, fuck it, it was fun. I looked over before retaking my seat and smiled when I saw Tiny laughing at my antics.

I only wished that it was Hope laughing at me. I loved to make her laugh, and it felt like a massive accomplishment since she rarely did. Her smile lit up the venue better than the thousand-dollar lights that shined down on us.

After our set, Finn announced the Sirens, and we left the stage. The crowd was rowdy, their screams hitting the stage like a destructive sound wave. It was fucking beautiful, but when Hope and the girls moved to go on the stage, she didn't even look my way.

Maybe she didn't see me?

I didn't go back to my room. Instead, I found myself bouncing on the side stage, pumped and ready to play again. It sucked that we didn't have another show until the next day. Hell, I was even considering going on stage with the girls, taking Hope's sticks, and going to town with her.

She looked fucking hot in her jeans and a Wonder Woman T-shirt. It wasn't anything fancy, but she made jeans and a T-shirt look sexy. The way the fabric clung to her sweaty body, showing the dips and curves of her athletic frame.

It wouldn't be long, and I'd have her beneath me. I'd dive into her depths, plunging hard and fast until she screamed my name and begged me to stop. I could hardly wait.

I nodded my head to the music as they played, my meds giving me a high like I hadn't felt in weeks. I sang along to the tune and used my drumsticks on anything close to me as I beat out the same beats that Hope was playing.

"You're in a better mood," Finn said at my side.

I nodded.

"I thought you went back to the hotel to talk to Faith?"

"I did, but she had to go. Baby boy got sick. She's going to call later."

"Is he okay?" I looked away from Hope to see a haggard Finn standing at my side.

I knew how hard it was for the boys to be away from their families, but it started to show in the lines around their eyes and the sadness in their smiles.

"Yeah, she said it's a stomach bug." He sighed and ran his hands through this hair. "Man, I hate being away from them. I hate that she's there by herself dealing with this shit. I hate to say this, but I'll be glad when this tour is over."

I didn't respond.

I couldn't say the same, but for reasons I'd never admit aloud. Being done with the tour meant not having an excuse to see Hope every day, and as lame as it sounded, I was enjoying her way too much already. I could only imagine how good it would be when we were finally fucking.

I really needed to snap out of it, and something told me the minute I stuck my dick in her, all the crazy thoughts running through my mind would go away. The need to be near her would dissolve, and she'd just be another girl I slept with. But before I could do that, I had to make it clear that it was a one-time thing, and I had to make sure she was okay with that.

When their set was over, they left the stage in a rush. The crew ushered them down the hallway toward the exit, where they would get in an SUV and be driven back to the hotel. Again, Hope didn't look at me. It was more than obvious now that she was ignoring me. I wasn't about to let that happen. I had plans with her and her body, so I wasn't about to let her shut me out when I was so close to getting what I wanted.

I went back to my room and showered quickly. I knew the routine. After a show, we all went out for drinks and food. I wanted to be alone with her and talk to her before we went out for the night … before the drinks. I needed her to have a clear head when I finally got her to agree to a night of mind-blowing sex with me.

Once I was dressed, I grabbed my wallet from the dresser, shoved it in my back pocket, and left for Hope's room. Things had to move quickly since I knew the girls would be tapping on her door soon.

She opened the door with a smile that disappeared when she saw me on the other side of the door. Her hair was wet, and her clothes stuck to her moist skin. The smell of her shampoo and soap rushed my senses, making me dizzy to taste her.

"You're ignoring me," I said, not beating around the bush since I knew I was limited on time.

"No, I'm not."

"And now you're lying."

She was a shitty liar. I couldn't blame her, really. I was a shitty liar, too … mostly because I never lied. I never really needed to until recently.

"What do you want, Chet?"

She rested the side of her face against the door, keeping it open just enough so that I was able to see the side of her body.

"After yesterday, it should be obvious what I want."

"I don't know what you're talking about." She closed the door a tiny bit more.

She knew exactly what I was talking about. I could see it in her eyes and how she stiffened at my words. Her actions were pissing me off, but two could play that game.

I pressed on the door, pushing it open and forcing her back until there was enough space for me to step into her room.

"What the fuck, Chet?" she yelled.

I slammed the door behind me and moved into her space. "Cut the shit. I don't have time for your bullshit games." My words came out a little too brash, but I no longer cared. I knew the girls would be beating on her door in just minutes, and I'd have to hand her over. I wanted to make a few things clear before that happened.

"I think the only person playing bullshit games is you."

She backed away from me, but I followed her step for step.

"Are you really going to act like the kiss didn't happen? Are you going to stand there and act like you didn't like it?" I moved closer until her back was against the wall opposite us, and I could press my body to hers. She pushed my chest to shove me away, but I didn't let her. "You're acting like your body wasn't crying for my touch. It was. I heard it screaming for me."

"Chet," she whispered as she once again attempted to push me away.

"Your nipples were so hard I could feel them against my chest." I brushed my thumb across her hardening nipple, and she gasped and grabbed my hand, twisting my fingers. "You want me, Hope, just admit it."

"S-stop," she stuttered.

"Stop what? Telling the truth?" I moved against her, forcing her tiny fingers into the skin of my chest. "Just admit it, Hope. You want me. You want to feel me moving inside you. You want me to make you come over and over again until you beg me to stop fucking you."

I was getting out of hand, and I knew that. What had started out as an innocent flirting session to turn her mind away from trying to ignore me and remember last night's kiss was slowly turning into something more.

My cock was hard and throbbing—trying to get to her—wanting to feel the inner walls of her sweet pussy clenching and pulling as it tugged an orgasm so intense from my body that even I'd cry out in pleasure.

83

Fuck.

This wasn't going as planned. This wasn't supposed to be happening. I knew the girls would be at her door any minute, and while we were both consenting adults, I knew one hint that anyone outside this room knew what was going on, and Hope would pull away from me. I knew how women worked, and while she was different from the rest, there were still some similarities.

Still, I couldn't stop rocking my hips into her and enjoying the feel of my cock nestled between her thighs.

"I'm warning you," she whispered, her voice breaking over her words.

Her cheeks were flushed, her ivory skin transforming to a pinkish tint before my eyes.

I would have never thought it, but I was breaking through Hope's walls, and it was easy. I thought this would be hard, but after the kiss and seeing the chills on her skin and the blush working its way into her shirt, she could no longer hide her little secret. And that secret was she wanted me.

It was the biggest ego boost ever.

The woman who had made her distaste for me so apparent for months was also attracted to me.

My hips thrust once again, my cock pressing into her, letting her know precisely how turned on I was.

"Chet, please," she choked.

My eyes moved from hers down to her plump lips. I wanted to taste her again. Once more wouldn't kill anyone. I wasn't much for kissing, but I'd kissed her so fucking hard, and I'd liked it. Standing there, looking down at Hope and her sweet mouth, I wanted nothing more than to kiss her—to open her mouth with mine and tongue fuck her senseless.

I moved in, my nose catching the side of her neck as I breathed in her freshly showered scent. "I love how you beg."

She swallowed hard, and I felt it against my lips.

"Seriously," she whispered, trying to push me away. "Please."

I looked up, and my eyes caught hers.

"Please what, Hope?" My fingers teased the bottom hem of her shirt and danced over the waist of her jeans.

I wanted her naked in bed.

I wanted her spread open for me.

I'd pushed myself too far, and I couldn't go back. I was fucking Hope, and I wasn't going to stop until she begged me—until I unloaded deep inside her wet cunt.

I reached out for the button of her jeans, and she grabbed my wrist, stopping me. Her nails dug into my skin, stinging with pleasure and making me hope she would dig them into my back until she drew blood.

I swallowed, my throat thick with want. "Let me touch you. I just want to touch you." I moved in and brushed my lips across the corner of hers. "Please," I whispered against her lips.

I'd never begged a woman before, but it had been so long, and I wanted her so badly.

Her grip loosened with the word *please*, and I went to work on the button of her jeans, pushing them apart until the zipper moved down on its own. Once I could, I shoved my hand inside her panties until I felt wet heat meet my fingertips.

She was so fucking wet and ready. She wanted me, and I was all about giving the ladies what they wanted.

Hope

My body was a traitorous whore ... slowly melting beneath Chet's nimble fingers. He knew what he was doing for sure. I'd only ever been with Chet, and it was only the one time, so my body was crying for someone other than myself to give me relief. It was shocking, but Chet was better at touching me than I was at touching myself.

I masturbated a lot.

I didn't trust anyone else to touch me.

I'd close my eyes and finger myself until my thighs would lift from the bed, and I could barely contain the noises spilling from my mouth. It was my way of dealing. It was my way of striking Chet from my body's memory—of wiping clean the beautiful things he'd done to me all those years ago, but what he was doing—the way he was touching me—was magical.

His finger rolled over my swollen clit, and I moaned.

"You like that?" he asked.

Again, he rolled his finger over my nub, and instead of moaning, I bit my lip until I was sure I was going to break the skin.

"Say you like it," he demanded.

The last thing I wanted him to do was to stop. I hated myself for melting for him, but it felt so fucking good. My hips jerked, pressing my pussy into his hand.

"I like it," I conceded.

I wasn't very good at fighting our little war. Just a simple touch of his fingers, and I was already waving the white flag. Hell, I wasn't waving it. I was wrapping myself in it.

His finger shifted, moving from my clit and down my slit until he teased my opening. My pussy clenched, begging him to stick his finger deep inside, but he continued to massage the rim, collecting my wetness and moving it all around.

"Please," I begged.

I fucking begged.

How could I sink so low?

How could I let this happen?

And with Chet fucking Rhodes, no less!

Imagining the real thing and having the real thing were two very different situations. I didn't know what it was about my obsession with Chet. I only knew I was beyond attracted to him ... I always had been. I knew I longed for every touch he was placing against my heated skin, but I also knew my hatred for him was still thriving—growing—expanding inside me until I wasn't sure there would be enough room for everything that I was and my abhorrence for him.

I was supposed to be moving past the past, but having him touch me and still not remember me made me angry. It didn't make any sense, but in my mind, it did. On the one hand, his lost memories of me were a good thing for the tour. It meant I could breeze through without having to explain my past to anyone.

On the other hand, it made me so angry I wanted to scream. How could he not remember our night together? I remembered every second—every touch—every word. It was making me crazy.

I was about to tell him to stop. I was about to rip his hands from my body and tell him to get the fuck out of my room, but he moved his hand, and a second finger joined the first before he pushed them deep inside me.

My head fell back against the wall. My breath rushed from my body so fast I was getting lightheaded. Sensations and pleasure struck me deep with each thrust of his fingers. And when his thumb moved over my clit, the pleasure only intensified.

"Oh, fuck." I opened my legs wider, giving him all of me.

He continued to curl his fingers into me, the pads of his fingertips teasing my G-spot and his thumb rolling over my clit until I felt my orgasm build.

"As soon as I make you come with my fingers, I'm going to fuck you up against this wall." He tapped the wall with his free hand. "I'm going to fuck you so hard you scream. Do you hear me, Hope?"

I heard him.

I heard every fucking word, and with every word, my impending orgasm grew.

"Yes. I-I hear you," I stuttered.

"Good. Now, fucking come on my fingers and pretend they're my cock."

My body lowered onto his curled fingers the more I spread my legs. I hadn't even realized it, but already one of my legs was free from my jeans, allowing me to open for him wider and wider.

He didn't let up, his fingers thrusting into me in perfect rhythm, his thumb teasing my swollen clit until I felt like I would explode. My body reacted to him—danced to his rhythm—until my orgasm was spreading into my thighs and ready to leak from my body.

"Don't stop," I breathed. "Fuck, Chet. Don't stop."

I sounded needy. I hated that, but at the same time, I was pretty sure I'd die if he stopped. I hadn't felt pleasure this potent in years. My body thanked me for giving in while my mind was cursing me.

He sped up, sensing my impending release, which was all it took. My body stiffened, and my mouth fell open. I gripped his shoulders, my nails digging into him, as I cried out with so much pleasure, my body began to tremble.

He kept moving—plunging his fingers into me until my body was jerking and twitching, and I was mumbling for him to stop. Cold air rushed into me when he pulled his fingers free, and before I could speak, he shoved his wet fingers into my mouth.

My flavor rolled over my tongue, and I sucked, tasting myself all over his thick fingers. Then he leaned in and stuck his tongue in my mouth with his fingers, lapping at my flavor like a starving man.

"Mmm," he moaned. "Fuck, you taste good."

My thighs clenched together, moisture pooling in my folds and sending slick sensations over my pleasure spots.

I should have stopped things then, but I couldn't. My body was greedy, and I wanted more. No matter how much I tried to deny it, I needed more.

Chet pushed my jeans down over my other leg until I was free from them, and then he tossed them across the room. My heart was slamming against my ribs as a quick list of consequences rushed through my memory.

I needed to stop this.

Why couldn't I stop this?

His fingers curled into the lace at the top of my underwear, and then he pulled, snapping them from my body with a loud pop. He grinned down at me with his crooked smile, my favorite, and even though I wanted to, I didn't smile back. I was naked from the waist down, exposed to the man I hated the most, and I couldn't find it in myself to care.

His hand moved down my side, guided it between my thighs, and he pinched my clit, making me gasp.

"Ready?" he asked.

I didn't respond.

I couldn't.

His belt clicked as he unbuckled it; his eyes glued to mine as if he dared me to stop him. Then he pushed his jeans down, and his hard, hot cock was pressing into my stomach.

He lifted me, his right hand curling around my left thigh and lifting it around his hip.

This was really happening. I was about to be fucked by Chet yet again. I could hardly believe I was letting this happen, but for the life of me, I couldn't stop it.

The head of his cock teased my clit before moving down my slit and nestling close to my entrance. One shift of his hips, and he'd be inside me, but before he could move, a loud banging sounded on my door.

We both stiffened, everything stopping and becoming so quiet, I could hear the outside world through the windows of my room.

"Open the fucking door, Hope; we're starving," Mia called through the door.

Again, they knocked, the sound echoing throughout the room.

"Don't move," Chet whispered. "They'll go away. This is happening."

His eyes devoured mine, daring me to speak or move, but reality came crashing down on me with each of their knocks. I couldn't let him fuck me. He'd had me so fucking turned on that I had almost let it happen … again.

What the fuck was wrong with me?

I shifted in his grasp, my pussy accidentally rubbing up against his cock, and he gasped before setting his head against my shoulder.

"Let me go," I said, pushing against his shoulder as I settled back onto my own two feet.

He threw his head back with a sigh as he let me go and stepped away. His belt jingled when he tugged his jeans back up around his hips and buttoned and zipped them.

While he did that, I ran around the room collecting my things, and dressing like a tornado was about to hit the hotel. The girls continued to knock.

"I'm coming!" I called out, hoping that would cease the knocking.

"No, but you were about to again," Chet muttered as he sat on my bed.

"What are you doing?" I whispered. "Get up and hide."

"What are we, fucking teenagers now? I'm not hiding. Let them think whatever the fuck they want."

And then, as if realizing that the door wasn't closed all the way, Lena came bursting into the room.

"Hope, what the hell? We're ready to ...."

Her words stopped when her eyes landed on Chet sitting on my bed. The rest of the girls followed her, their eyes growing large when they too realized that Chet Rhodes was lounging on my bed.

It couldn't have looked good ... especially since as they walked in, I was buttoning my jeans.

Fucking great.

"Did we interrupt?" Mia asked with a grin.

"Yeah, you kind of did," Chet said.

"No!" I shouted over him.

Chet stood with a chuckle.

"Thanks a lot, girls," he said to the group as he made his way through them and to the door. He turned around and faced me before exiting. "I'll see you later, and we'll finish what we started."

And then he was gone, leaving me in a room full of girls with their eyes wide in shock and big grins plastered across their faces.

"Let's go." I changed the subject. "I'm starving."

I moved to walk toward the door, but Twiggy stopped me with a hand on my arm.

"Oh no, ma'am, we aren't going anywhere until you tell us everything."

12

CHET

Sitting across the room from Hope while everyone ate and drank was driving me fucking crazy. My dick had barely gone down, and every time she looked at me, it would harden all over again.

Every time I closed my eyes, I could still see her face as she came all over my fingers. I could still smell her there every time I lifted my drink to my lips, and even hours later, her flavor was still thick on my tongue.

She could run, but she couldn't hide. I'd get her alone again, and when I did, I was sinking so deep into her I'd get lost. I wanted her as badly as I wanted my Blackbird. I'm not sure how it was possible to long for two women in the same manner, but I did.

It wasn't like with the rest of the women. I felt a deep ache in my chest. I wanted Hope and Blackbird differently than I'd wanted any other woman. I couldn't explain it, but it settled in my stomach like weighted sands, making me feel irrational and crazy.

There was no telling where Blackbird was these days, but I knew I'd left her in South Carolina. I'd go back once this tour was over. I'd go home and see if I could find the guy I was with her five years before ... the same guy who seemed to come out and play whenever he was alone with Hope.

I liked being him. I liked the way I felt when I was him. Maybe that was why I was so obsessed with Blackbird, and now, obsessed with being with Hope.

My drink burned the back of my throat when I took a large gulp. Across the room, Hope's eyes were all over me, taunting me and making me hard all over again.

Tonight.

She would be mine tonight.

13

HOPE

"**A** re you fucking him?" Mia asked.

"Is he as good in bed as he claims he is?" Lena questioned before I could even answer Mia. "He walks around like he has a golden cock that won't stop."

"Please tell me you're not fucking him." Constance pinched the bridge of her nose and sighed. "He's not the kind of guy to double-dip, Hope, and I just don't want to see you get hurt."

Twiggy laughed. "She said double dip."

Mia and Lena laughed along with them. At this point, I still hadn't spoken. I was too busy thinking of a lie ... trying to think of a reason for Chet Rhodes to be in my room.

And then it hit me.

"He just had some questions about my set," I lied.

"Did those questions require you to unbutton your jeans because you were totally buttoning them when we walked in," Mia said. "Oh, my God, you said your set. You don't have a set of balls hanging between your legs that we don't know about, do you?"

"I definitely think Chet would go both ways," Twiggy pondered.

"My fucking drum set, Mia. I don't have balls!"

The conversation was getting out of hand. I needed to nip it in the bud and get us moving.

"Can we please go eat now? I'm starving." I moved toward the door, hoping the girls would follow.

"Yeah, starving for Chet's cock," Twiggy muttered behind her hand, making Mia and Lena chuckle.

"That's enough, girls," Constance interrupted. "Hope isn't fucking Chet, and even if she were, it's not our fucking business. Now, come on. Let's go eat."

• • • ● • ● ● • • •

Chet didn't take his eyes off me all night. I tried to eat, but my food kept sticking to the roof of my mouth, making it nearly impossible to swallow. So I gave up on eating, and instead, I drank and tried to keep my eyes away from him.

He sat across the room, drinking with his sexy grin and telling me with his eyes that he wasn't finished with me yet. Every now and again, he'd run his fingers under his nose and close his eyes in pleasure. He was smelling me on his fingers and enjoying it, and honestly, it turned me on.

The way he had worked me over, making me come so hard, was marked in my memory. And even with loud music and the group around me talking loudly, I was still replaying that moment in my mind, getting myself worked up without even being touched.

The night stretched out, and the longer I sat there and felt Chet's eyes all over me, the wetter I got. The wetter I got, the more uncomfortable it became to be wearing jeans with no underwear... thanks to Chet. Knowing him, he'd probably stuffed them in his pocket.

The longer I sat there, the more I no longer cared about anything else but feeling him move inside me. I was clenching my thighs together and enjoying the sensation while everyone else around me, minus Chet, was utterly clueless.

The night wound down, and we took our SUVs back to the hotel. The girls stuck by my side like they knew what I was thinking. I was thinking I hoped Chet followed me to my room. I hoped he came to my room and fucked me all night long, but that couldn't happen if the girls were with me every second.

Relief washed over me when we went separate ways after stepping off the elevator. The girls giggled down the hall to their rooms, and I smiled and shook my head as I slipped the card key into the slot. The door clicked, and the green light flashed, but before I could push the door open, heat washed over my back, and a hand slid around my waist.

"What are you doing?" I asked.

I didn't have to turn around to know it was Chet. His familiar scent moved over me, and I breathed deeply, storing the moment in my long-term memory.

"Finishing what we started," he muttered against my neck, making the hair on my arms prickle.

He pushed down on the knob, and the door popped open. The room was dim, the bathroom light cutting a line across the entrance. My knees wobbled when I stepped over the threshold, and he followed me in, closing the door behind us and locking it.

"No fucking interruptions," he said.

My brain buzzed with the drinks I'd sipped all night, and even though I was running the reasons I shouldn't go through with this through my mind, I couldn't stop my body from responding when he moved behind me and caught my hips in his hands. His lips brushed the back of my neck, and I exhaled loudly.

"I think I want to fuck you from behind. How does that sound?"

His whispered words shifted the hairs on the back of my neck, and I shivered.

I nodded. "Yes."

No.

No.

No.

Consequences.

But one time couldn't hurt. Just once more, and I'd never let him touch me again. I wanted to feel him, and after I soothed the ache, I'd remain friendly, but I'd stay away until the tour was over.

"Just once to get it out of our system," I informed him.

I wanted to make sure he understood this wouldn't happen again. He needed to know that this was a one-time thing. Not that I had too much to worry about. Like Constance had said, Chet wasn't the kind to double-dip. So maybe all this reassurance was for myself. Maybe I was the one who needed to hear that it was only going to happen once and never again.

"Just once," he agreed.

And then he was moving me across the room to the hotel desk. He rolled the desk chair out of the way and pressed my hipbones into the hard wood. His finger deftly unbuttoned my jeans before he tugged them down over my hips.

His belt buckle sounded behind me, and then he was pressing against my back and bending me over the desk. His hot skin pressed against my ass, his hard cock resting between my ass cheeks. His hand slid over my hip, across my pelvic bone, and down until his fingers teased my clit.

His other hand cupped my throat, pulling me back enough to see our reflections in the mirror in front of the desk.

"Look at me. I want to see your face when I push inside you."

My eyes caught his in the reflection as he slid into me from behind, slow and deep. My eyes fluttered closed at the sweet sensation of him filling me.

"No, baby, keep them open."

I saw his strained expression when I looked at him in the mirror, and I could tell it was killing him to take it slow. Slow wasn't what I wanted, either. I wanted him to fuck me—slam his body into mine so hard it hurt—so fast I shook with pleasure.

"Fuck me," I demanded.

The side of his mouth lifted in his sexy grin, and the hand he had around my throat tightened. His hips shifted, and he began to pound into me, slamming his cock into my tight, wet passage so hard and fast my stomach clenched from the sensation.

"Like this?" he asked. "Is that how you want it?"

I tried to drop my head, the pleasure making my body go loose, but he jerked my head back up, and his hand tightened once again around my throat.

"Look at me when I'm fucking you," he growled.

The desk shook, my hips bones digging into the sharp edge. His hips worked quickly, his length filling me deeply with each thrust until I felt an ache building inside me. With one hand still on my throat squeezing, he used his free hand to finger me, rolling my swollen clit between his fingers and pinching with just a touch of pain.

I looked him in the eye, his fierce expression almost deadly while he fucked me. It was different than that first time together. It wasn't slow. It wasn't easy. It was hard and fast, while he tightened his chokehold and abused my clit.

I loved every fucking second.

My pussy tightened as the hand around my throat tightened, and when my orgasm rolled over me, he squeezed harder, cutting off the blood flow and making my mind spin with my release. I couldn't scream out. I couldn't moan. I couldn't do anything but let my body take control and let my release crash over me like a wave of humidity and pleasure so intense I shook.

"Yeah, that's it," Chet muttered in my ear. "Fuck, your pussy's so tight when you come."

And then his squeeze hold around my throat loosened. The blood rushed to my brain, and oxygen flooded my lungs, and I went crazy, backing my ass into his thrusts and clawing at his naked hips for more.

"Harder," I demanded. "Fuck me harder!"

He pulled from my body and turned me so fast I went dizzy. My jeans tangled around my ankles, and I stepped on them and pulled until my feet were free and I could move.

Chet moved me away from the desk, picked me up as if I weighed nothing, and tossed me onto the bed. His stern expression went darker as he climbed on top of me, spread my legs, and thrust his cock into me hard and fast.

He pounded into me, pushing my body across the bed until my head hung off the side. Again, he worked my body until I was on the brink of coming. Tugging at his arm at the side of my head, I placed his hand around my throat and pressed his fingers into my skin.

His fingers tightened around my throat, squeezing so hard I could feel my pulse banging against his fingers. With my head over the side of the bed and his chokehold, everything stopped except the orgasm that was building in my core.

His hips moved faster, his stern facial expressions going slack as pleasure overtook him. His mouth hung open, and knowing that my body was making him feel good made my orgasm rush to a head.

I came hard, screaming inside even though I couldn't make any noise. And as my inner muscles tightened around him, I watched with wide eyes as he bit his bottom lip and lost total control.

I'd never seen Chet so wild. I'd never seen him so crazy. He thrust into me like a beast on a mission, his hand moving from my throat and to the mattress to hold him above me as his hips took over completely.

"Oh fuck, baby," he gasped with closed eyes. "Goddamn, Hope."

His moan was loud and followed by a growl as he burst inside me. His perfect rhythm became uncoordinated and uneven, slowing as he released and slumped over me. His chest and stomach pressed into mine as his body dropped, and his weight pressed me into the mattress.

His face rested against my neck, making his heated breaths rush against my skin and sending chills through my exhausted body.

I was relaxed, my muscles going limp from the strenuous releases Chet had given me. He'd made good on his promise. He'd fucked me hard and fast, and he'd made me come until I was on the brink of begging him to stop.

Cool air rushed over my naked bottom when he pulled from my body and rolled over onto his side. My shirt was twisted around my waist, and I tugged it down over my hips.

"That was fucking amazing," he breathed into the dim space around us.

I stared at the ceiling as euphoria slowly melted away, and realization moved into its space.

What had I done?

What was I thinking?

Panic consumed me, and I began to freak out. I was lying next to Chet Rhodes after the best sex I'd had in my life, and all I could think about were the consequences of what we'd done.

And no matter what, I knew there'd be consequences because already, as I lay there in silence and listened to his breathing even out, all the feelings I'd kept tucked away were rushing to the forefront and demanding to be felt.

This wasn't good. It wasn't something I would let happen. Chet didn't know what it meant to have feelings. I'd seen how he worked, and I knew what he was about.

A one-time thing.

I'd set the rules, and he would play by them, and I knew as I slowly drifted off to sleep that it would hurt like hell when he didn't break that rule the way he broke all the rest.

14

CHET

I woke with a hammer in my head, beating against my brain with force like never before. I blinked up at the dark ceiling, feeling disoriented and confused.

My migraine was so extreme that I instantly felt nauseated. I pushed up onto my elbows, and as the room came into focus, I was reminded of where I'd fallen to sleep.

Hope.

I'd been inside Hope, and holy shit, she was everything I'd expected and more. And after going weeks without sex, I didn't think I'd ever stop coming once I started. She was a champ, taking my rough thrusts and begging me for more. She wanted it harder, and I'd given her just that until my hips ached, and I couldn't hold back any longer.

I climbed from her bed, careful not to wake her, and adjusted my jeans. I stood above her, watching her sleep. She was shivering, half of her body naked and covered in chills. The comforter was soft in my grasp as I pulled it over her round hips and perfect thighs.

Damn, she was beautiful.

Every inch of her.

I grinned when she snuggled into the blanket and turned onto her side.

I'd promised one time and one time only, but I wasn't so sure it was a promise I could keep. Fucking any woman more than once wasn't something I often did, but I think as long as I knew Hope was like me, unable to develop feelings, I could see myself pushing inside her once more.

The hallway was empty, everyone in the hotel sleeping since it was almost morning. My room was dark, but I could get to the desk, which housed an unopened water bottle. Pulling the tiny bottle of prescription painkillers from my back pocket, I dumped three into my palm, tossed them into my mouth, and took a few swigs from the water bottle to wash them down.

The pressure and pain digging into my brain felt like the roof pushing down on me. It was getting worse, but I knew I could make it through the end of the tour. I'd worry about the rest at the end of the tour. I'd go back to the doctors and figure out how to keep myself comfortable until the end, which was obviously approaching.

I lay in my bed, staring at the ceiling and waiting for the pills to take me away. All I could think about was Hope and how amazing she'd felt ... how sexy she'd looked when she came all over my cock.

My body was relaxing, having been thoroughly drained. My muscles ached, and I was sated in a way I hadn't been since the beginning of the tour when Ass Fingerer had sucked my load down her throat.

My body relaxed into the mattress, my breathing evening out with the relief of my pain pills dissolving my migraine. And as I slipped into a deep sleep, I smiled to myself because I knew it didn't matter what promises I had made to Hope.

I'd have her again.

Finally, I fell asleep, and a dream much better than any reality welcomed me. A threesome with Hope and Blackbird, both women moaning in pleasure as one sat on my face and the other rode my cock. I licked and sucked, moaning into her soft folds as the other bounced on my dick, making my balls clench in pleasure.

Then a loud knock sounded on the door, and my eyes flew open. The sun beat into my eyes, taunting the edges of a promising migraine.

"Go the fuck away," I yelled, turning onto my side and covering my head with my pillow.

The door opened, letting me know I hadn't closed it all the way the night before.

"Rise and shine, Princess," Zeke sang as he jumped on my bed. "It's time to eat, Chet. Get the fuck up."

I loved my boys, I really did, but when I opened my eyes and looked up to see them standing above me with well-rested smiles, I wanted to kick their asses.

It would have to be another day because, well ... bacon.

We played our final show in Houston and went to what was labeled as the best steakhouse in Texas afterward for dinner. My migraine had returned during the show, forcing me to take two more pills during a short set break.

I swallowed the pills and rested my head against the snare drum as Finn talked to the crowd and got them rowdy. Their screams only made the pain in my head pound harder, but I had to finish the tour. Once I finished the tour, whatever was going to happen could happen.

The group around me ate and joked while I shifted the food around my plate, suddenly feeling nauseated by every aroma in the room. Thankfully, no one mentioned it, and I was able to sit back and sip my beer in peace.

Hope sat down the table from me, and every now and again, I could feel her eyes on me—watching me. She knew something was wrong, but I refused to look at her. I knew once I did, I'd never make it to my room without going to hers first.

For the first time in my life, I wasn't sure I could even get it up, much less perform. My head was hurting so badly, and no matter how many pain pills I took, it wasn't letting up.

The ride to the hotel was quiet; the boys said nothing as the SUV cut through the Houston traffic. I stared out the window, watching the cars go by, and wondered how much longer I had.

Months?

Weeks?

Days?

Or hours?

It was the not knowing that was bothering me, not death itself.

"On the road in the morning," Finn muttered as he unlocked his hotel room door and opened it.

"Here we come, New Orleans," I responded with a grin I didn't actually feel.

I stuck my card key in the lock and opened the door when it clicked.

"Hey, Chet," Finn said, stopping me from entering my room.

"Yeah?"

"Whatever it is, I'm here, man."

My throat closed as sadness swooped over me. I couldn't respond; my words wouldn't move past the lump lodged in my throat. Instead, I nodded and went into my room, closing the door behind me.

Sleep didn't come, even though I'd taken enough meds to put down two men. The ceiling loomed above me, sometimes looking like it was lowering, ready to suffocate me.

Thoughts of Hope lingered, and when I closed my eyes, her memories brought a sense of relief and calm. I could hear her laughter from earlier in the night, and I set it on replay in my memory. The moans she made when I entered her, the look in her eyes when she came.

If lying there thinking about her brought me relief, what would the actual act do?

I sat up, my head feeling like I'd slammed it against a wall as the blood rushed out. The room spun around me, and I didn't know if it was the migraine or the pills that were the cause.

It was three in the morning, and we would be getting on the bus and heading to New Orleans at seven, but I needed to see her. I didn't like feeling so needy when it came to seeing a woman, but fuck it. Whatever gave me relief ... and Hope did precisely that.

When I was focusing on her and giving her pleasure, I wasn't thinking about dying or the pain that came with it. So I'd go to Hope and bury myself inside her. If I couldn't get hard, I'd taste her, finger fuck her, whatever took my focus away from the pain and put it entirely on her and making her feel good.

Sure, I'd said one time only, but I'd never been one to follow the rules. I was a rebel, and everyone who knew me knew that. But when it came to Hope and the way she made me feel, I'd break every fucking rule in the book and then some.

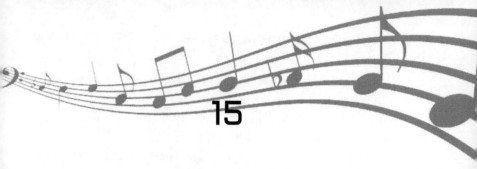

15

Hope

We were getting on the road at seven, and I knew I needed to sleep, but I couldn't. All I could think about was Chet and how he was acting at dinner. We had agreed on a one-time thing, but I couldn't help but feel a little let down that he hadn't come to the room.

He did something to me—changed me—and turned on a light inside me during sex. I'd actually enjoyed being choked. It intensified my orgasm, making me come so hard it paralyzed me.

He was good in bed.

No.

He was amazing in bed.

I should have known then that one time would never be enough, but I couldn't take any chances. Already, I found myself thinking about him more. Lying there, I wondered what he was doing ... wondering if he was with another woman or a group of women.

I hated myself for thinking these things, but Chet did that to me. He did that to me five years before, and it was happening again. I knew it would be this way, and still, I'd let it happen. I was weak. I'd always been weak.

Giving up on sleep, I climbed from my bed and turned on the TV. An old episode of *Golden Girls* lit up the screen. We didn't have a show for a few days, which meant I didn't need to be well-rested. Good thing, since sleep obviously wasn't coming for me.

I settled into the comforter and rested against the bed's headboard. Lights from the TV danced around the room, flickering across the walls and taking away the darkness around me.

Finally, my eyes grew heavy, and my body began to relax. Sleep was moving over me, granting me the solace I'd been asking for since I woke up to find Chet gone from my bed.

He'd crept from my bed in the night, leaving me feeling slightly used and extremely relieved. It was the strangest situation. I wanted him there, but I wanted him gone. It was like I was two different women. One begging for him and the other pushing him away with fear that he'd suddenly remember our night five years ago.

I couldn't relive the weeks after that night again. I didn't even want to think about what had happened in the months after I'd left Chet's room. The pain—the heartache—the death of a young girl ... me. Or at least the girl I used to be. She was gone, and all that was left was me.

I could decorate my outer shell with all the color and life I wanted, but inside, I was just black sadness. Thick with memories and emotions I worked every day to forget. When I was with Chet, the inside matched the outside. The blackness became bright, and the memories were chased away into the corners of my mind. That was what he did to me, and that was why he was so addictive.

I jumped when a knock sounded on my door. I was on my toes, creeping across the room to the door, when the second knock sounded. The door was cold against my face when I pressed my eye to the peephole.

Chet stood there. He ran his fingers through his hair in aggravation. He looked like he was in pain, which was the only reason I opened the door ... at least, that was what I told myself as I reached out and unlocked it. As soon as I opened the door, his expression changed, and instead of pain, a sexy grin tilted his lips.

My eyes moved over him, taking in his naked chest and wide, thick shoulders. My body responded immediately to him.

"Are you going to let me in?" he asked.

I stepped to the side, giving him space to step into the room. It was then that I realized what I was wearing. A thin Guns-N-Roses T-shirt and a pair of panties. The shirt was long enough to cover me, but it was not like it mattered. He'd already seen everything I had to offer down south anyway.

"What do you want, Chet?" I closed the door behind him and set the lock.

When I turned around, his eyes were on my legs and slowly rising, taking me in and making me feel completely exposed.

"I think you know the answer to that already." He sucked his bottom lip into his mouth, his teeth raking over his lip rings.

He grabbed my hand, pulling me into him and holding me close in an unexpected move. His arms tightened around me, and his lips moved to my neck, sending heated chills over my skin.

"Chet," I whispered.

He didn't respond. Instead, his lips moved up over my chin to my lips. I kissed him back, letting him take control of my mouth and move me across the room toward the bed.

The lights from the TV grew brighter, flickering over the bed like a directional beacon.

"I thought we said just once," I said against his mouth.

He pulled away, and his eyes moved to mine. His grin was devious. "Fuck the rules." His fingers snagged the elastic waist of my panties, and he began to push them down over my hips. His eyes remained on mine, daring me to stop him. "I wanna be inside you."

I caught my lips between my teeth to stop my smile. "And what about what I want?"

He pulled back, tugged his pajama bottoms down, revealing his hard cock, and grasped his shaft.

With confusion on his face, like he couldn't imagine a woman not wanting him, he asked, "You don't want this?"

He pumped himself in his grasp, the tip of his cock growing before my eyes and the piercing at the tip shining in the flickering lights of the TV.

I had to taste him.

I'd thought about doing it over the years, wishing I'd taken the opportunity five years ago. But he was there, and he was offering himself. I planned to take full advantage even though I knew it was the last thing I should do.

I dropped to my knees in front of him, grabbed his cock, and covered the tip with my mouth. His piercing tapped against my back teeth before rubbing the back of my throat. His fingers dove into my hair, fingering the strands as I began to suck him off. I'd never done it before, and I was sure my inexperience showed, but I didn't care. I wanted to taste him, and he tasted amazing.

His thumb softly skimmed the skin beside my mouth.

"Yes. That feels so fucking good, baby."

His words pushed me, and I sucked harder, working my hand up and down the shaft the way I'd seen the girls do in the porn movies I'd watched. I must have been doing it right because the sounds he made were perfection.

I could feel his moans between my legs, making me grow wet and turning my clit into a hard, aching pebble.

"Fuck this," he growled, sliding his cock from my mouth.

He reached down and helped me stand, and then he tossed me onto the bed. I loved how he took control ... the way he prowled toward me before climbing over me. His lips skimmed my thigh, before moving over my T-shirt, until he was nibbling my chin and aggressively kissing me.

He roughly pushed my panties down the rest of the way until I could kick them from my feet, and the bed shook as he quickly got rid of his pants. He nudged my thighs open with his knee, and then he was inside me, taking what he wanted in the fast and rough style I loved.

My nails dug into his naked back, going deeper the harder he fucked me. Lifting my hips, I took all he had to offer. He felt so fucking good, hitting all my most sensitive spots and sending me spiraling before I even had a chance to climb to my climax.

I screamed, begging him to fuck me harder and faster while I came so hard my body began to shake. He didn't let up, even when his thrusts began pushing me across the bed until my head was once again hanging from the side.

He leaned over me, biting at my erect nipple through my T-shirt until he grew aggravated with the fabric in his way.

"Fuck this." His body slowed. "I want you naked."

He reached between us and grabbed at the hem of my shirt. "I want to suck your tits while I fuck you."

He was so blunt … so sure about what he wanted, and it was fucking hot. I didn't usually like giving up control of any aspect of my life, but when it came to having sex with Chet, his control made me feel safe. It made me hot—begging for more of his power—more of his body.

He lifted my shirt and ripped it over my head. His eyes landed on my chest, taking in my hard, erect nipples as his hand cupped my left breast. And then, as if he'd been struck by lightning, he jerked, and everything stopped.

He slid from my body and reached over, turning on the bedside lamp and illuminating the space around us. His eyes moved over my chest, wide and wild, as if he'd just discovered one of life's great mysteries. I wasn't sure what was happening, but the mood around us shifted.

His eyes moved from my chest and up my neck, and over my chin before clashing with mine. He stared into my eyes, confusion tugging at his dark brows.

"It's you," he said in awe.

I had no idea what he was talking about.

Suddenly, I was worried that maybe Chet was slipping into the same zone he'd been in, in the hotel hallway in Vegas.

The confusion.

The worry.

All the emotions that moved over his features were similar to those of the night before.

"What?" I asked.

"It's you. You're her." He wasn't making any sense.

"I don't know what you're talking about, Chet."

And I didn't.

Again, his eyes moved from mine and down over my chest.

"The blackbird tattoo," he mumbled. "It's different now, but that's definitely it."

I looked down at the tiny blackbird I had tatted on the space between my shoulder and the top of my right breast. I'd gotten it done years before, only weeks before my night with Chet. It marked the beginning of my rebellion—the beginning of the girl I'd become. It was a beacon for me, and I loved it.

I'd changed it a little over the years, adding the date of the worst day of my life beneath it, shading some rainbow coloring to the tips of the wings. But essentially, it had primarily stayed the same.

"What about it?" I asked, confused.

"It was you that night," he said, his eyes moving to mine. "You left. Why did you leave?"

And just like that, the room crumbled all around me.

No.

The entire hotel—the entire city of Houston—all crumbled, as the one thing I silently hoped wouldn't happen happened.

Chet was slowly remembering me.

He was remembering our night together all those years ago, and soon, he would have a ton of questions. Questions I wasn't sure I could answer.

I should have been happy that he remembered. I should have been glad that I wasn't just another woman he had fucked and forgotten, but I'd grown accustomed to him not remembering. I was comfortable with him because of my anonymity, but I no longer had that.

"Get off me," I barked, pushing at his chest until he lifted his body from mine and moved to my side.

"Hope?"

His confusion continued as he climbed from the bed and tugged his pants back on. His eyes never left my face. I could feel his gaze digging into my flesh, judging me, hating me.

I didn't look at him. Instead, I collected my T-shirt and panties and began to dress. I wanted him out of my room. I couldn't breathe with him there.

"Leave."

He crossed his arms, his expression changing from confused to angry.

"I'm not going anywhere."

I tugged my underwear over my hips, covering myself and hoping I wouldn't feel so exposed.

"I said get out of my room!"

"Not until we talk about that night. Not until I get some answers."

I moved, grabbing a pair of shorts from the top of the dresser and tugging them over my hips.

"Fine," I snapped. "Then I'll leave."

I started toward the door, ready to leave him standing in the middle of my room with all my belongings—all my secrets—but before I could get to the door, he grabbed my arm and pulled me to his chest. His body was hot and hard against mine, reminding me of the pleasure he'd just conjured from my body.

"I took your virginity, Hope. I've never done that with any other woman." His fingers dug into the tops of my arms, holding me in place and keeping me from fleeing.

"You didn't. It wasn't me. I don't know what you're talking about," I lied.

I tugged, his fingers bruising my arms as I tried to get away. He continued as if I hadn't spoken.

"The sex was amazing. You were amazing, but when I woke up, you were gone, and all that was left was a spot of blood on the sheets. What the fuck happened, Hope? I deserve to know!"

He was yelling.

His cheeks were red in anger, and his neck stiff and strained. He didn't deserve anything from me. I'd forgotten that while he was busy pleasuring me, but it was time that things went back to the way they were, if that were even possible now. It was time I stayed away from Chet, and he stayed away from me.

"I said," I bellowed in his face, "I don't know what the fuck you're talking about."

"You're lying." His eyes moved over my face, and he picked up a strand of my hair and held it up. "I can't believe I didn't see it sooner. I was so fucking drunk that night, but I remember now. It was you, and you know it. Tell me what happened, Hope." His voice softened to a deadly whisper.

I'd been around Chet for months. I'd seen him laugh and play. I'd seen him in a shitty mood. I'd seen him drunk and high. I'd watched him above me while he unloaded inside me. Hell, I'd seen him getting a blowjob with some bitch's finger up his ass, but I'd never seen him so angry ever.

His nostrils flared with each breath, and his eyes were red and watered down. His jaws clenched, making the muscles tic. He was about to explode, and I wasn't sure I wanted to be in the room when that happened.

I could handle a man like Chet, no problem. I knew how to use my fists and kick a man in the balls, but that didn't mean I wanted it to go that far. That didn't mean I didn't feel fear when he looked at me the way he was.

Still, that didn't keep me from screaming an answer in his face. He didn't need to know how badly he'd hurt me.

No.

He hadn't hurt me.

I'd hurt myself.

But I had to tell him something. I had to tell him anything that would make him let me go—anything that would make him forget about me again—make him go away.

Everything else, I'd keep locked away. The rest of my secrets were just that ... secrets, and I'd keep them until the day I died.

"I left because I was done with you," I lied. "I got what I wanted from you, and I left."

It wasn't true.

The truth was I woke up in his arms that night and felt something odd shift in my chest. He was spooning me, mumbling sweet nothings in my ear, and I knew ... I just fucking knew that I was in love with him. I'd been in love with him since the first time I'd laid eyes on him at The Pit, a hole-in-the-wall bar where he and the guys used to play.

But I also knew that Chet Rhodes would never settle down. I'd realized during our night together what kind of guy Chet was. I'd heard it whispered all around us at the party. I saw it in the way the other girls looked at me—as if they felt sorry for me—like I was stupid enough to think there would be more between us.

Even seeing all these things—hearing the things I'd heard—I still slept with him that night. I couldn't resist him. And when I woke up that morning, realizing how deep into Chet I was, I left.

It hurt to walk away from him. I'd walked around like a brokenhearted bitch for the following two weeks, but I did it to save myself a world of heartache. I did it to save myself from pain much worse than what I'd caused myself.

His expression shifted from anger to hurt before turning to anger once again. His grip on me loosened, and he moved away from me.

He believed me.

He believed my lies, and in a way, it pissed me off that he could ever think I'd be that kind of girl.

I'd given myself to him. I'd opened up to him in a way that I never had with another human being, and then I'd left. I could never be the kind of person I was portraying myself to be. I could have never used a guy for sex. Even thinking it made me sick to my stomach.

He moved farther away, his eyes glued to mine, and again, hurt seeped into his expression.

Hurting him was killing me, but I knew it was the right thing to do. I knew it was the only option. It would keep the peace for the rest of the tour, which was important. Not to mention, we could go right back to hating each other—ignoring each other—and being normal around each other. At least, I hoped we could.

Because of that, I let him walk away from me thinking that I was a dirty bitch—that I'd fucked him and chucked him as he had done to so many women before and after me. I let him think whatever he wanted, as long as things could return to the way they were.

I should have never let him touch me. I should have never let him in my room, but I had, and by doing so, I'd reset mentally and physically. I'd blown away all the work I'd put into myself to get over Chet and everything about him. But it was too late now. My body remembered him—longed for him—cried for him, and I couldn't do anything about it. I'd have to go cold turkey again. I'd done it before, and I could do it again.

I had to get Chet Rhodes out of my system. It was time I let the past go. It was time I moved on. I didn't care if I had to sleep with every man I passed, I'd get over the past, and I'd move past Chet. I'd let it all go, and I'd never think of him again the minute our tour was over.

I was done ... officially.

When he reached my door, he popped it open and let the cool air from the hallway into my still room. With his back to me, he stopped.

"You're a shitty liar, Hope," he muttered.

And then he left my room, slamming the door behind him and leaving me alone.

My legs gave out, and I sat on the bed, the soft cushion keeping me from hitting the floor.

It was over.

Everything was done.

I'd lied and saved myself heartache once more. It was the right thing to do. It was the smart thing to do. And from that moment on, I'd keep my distance from Chet. I'd do whatever it took to ensure he never caught me alone again. Because while I'd hoped to keep my white flag tucked away, never to be waved again, I knew I had no willpower when it came to him touching me.

16

CHET

Hope was Blackbird ... *my* Blackbird. The girl who had been on my mind for the past five years of my life—who had given me a night unlike any other night with a woman—was Hope.

Sure, we were young. Of course, I was totally wasted, but the more I closed my eyes and saw Hope's face, the more my memories with Blackbird came in clearly. I could hardly believe it, but I was slowly remembering everything about that night ... every second.

We hopped on the bus and pulled out for New Orleans at precisely seven in the morning. Keeping my distance from the rest of the guys, I lay in my bunk and thought about every detail I could have of Blackbird and Hope. It was definitely her.

We pulled into the New Orleans hotel six hours later, and within the hour, I was settled into my room. Technically, we only had one show in New Orleans, but everyone had decided that since we had a few days until our show in Florida, we were going to stay that few days drinking fishbowls on Bourbon Street and eating jambalaya.

But I didn't leave my room again until it was time to go on, and the guys didn't push. Instead, I ordered room service and swallowed as many pills as I could without killing myself. My migraine remained, but the medicine made it manageable.

The following day, we played a great show. I kept my head in the game, playing hard and ignoring the pounding in my head. Constance sat on the side stage watching the show, but the other girls stayed away. Secretly, I had hoped Hope would show up so I could see her. Just because I had stayed away from her didn't mean it was what I wanted. I wanted to see her.

No.

I needed to see her.

Because of that, I stood on the side stage and watched the Sirens play. Looking at Hope while she played the drums in front of a venue full of fans, I couldn't believe I hadn't seen it before. Sure, she had rainbow hair now instead of the long, dark locks. And sure, she didn't dress provocatively the way she had five years ago. She was the opposite of provocative, in fact, with her boyish jeans and graphic tees.

It was more than the way she dressed, though. More than her hair color. It was her face and her dark eyes that were capable of looking right through me. She did it that night five years ago, and she was doing it now.

It was glaringly obvious to me now.

How could I have missed it before?

Every time I closed my eyes, our night together came rushing back. My once blurred and drunken memories of her face—her smile—her eyes—were clear as day now.

Her laughter.

The way she'd come apart in my hands in her hotel room.

It all brought back memories of our night together.

For years, I'd longed for Blackbird. I'd longed to feel how she'd made me feel that night together. She made me feel like I was the only man in the world—like I was the only thing holding her to the planet. And for months, I'd been close to her, and the possibility of feeling that way again, and I'd had no idea.

Her behavior toward me made sense now that I knew the truth. No wonder she stayed away from me in the beginning. No wonder she'd pushed me away. I didn't understand her contempt since she was the one who walked away from me, but still, the last few months around her and the missing puzzles pieces were coming together.

I felt like the biggest dumbass ever. I was sure she had thought me an idiot on several occasions. A drunken playboy who slept with women and forgot about them the second they left. And while that was mostly true, it was different with her, and I needed to figure out a way to tell her that. I wanted to show her our situation was a unique one.

I was lost about many things when it came to Hope, but one thing was for sure... She was lying about her reasons for leaving that night.

I refused to believe that she had used me.

No.

I could remember the way she touched me. How inexperienced she was. How sweet and soft and amazing. There was no way she had used me for anything. The girl she was then could never, and something told me that even though she hid it well, that girl was still there. Locked behind rainbow hair and a bad attitude was my sweet Blackbird. And if it were the last thing I did in his life, I'd draw her out again.

When their show was over, I moved to the side and waited for the girls when they left the stage. They each acknowledged me as they ran toward the back of the venue. All except Hope.

She ran past me, her eyes never looking in my direction, even though I knew she knew I was there. I didn't like the game she was playing. I was about to go after her and demand that she give me the attention I was used to, but when I turned, Zeke was standing there looking back at me.

"We're ready to get the fuck out of here, man. We need real food. You coming or what?"

We had played a hard show, and I was beyond exhausted and starving. My headache had decided to return with a vengeance about thirty minutes into the Siren's show. I wanted to hang with the guys, especially to eat something that wasn't room service, but I wasn't up for anything.

"Nah, man, I'm good. Bring me back a burger or something."

I moved toward the back of the venue, prepared to go to the hotel and crash until we pulled out for the next city, but before I could get far, Zeke stopped me.

"What's up with you, Chet? You're acting fucked up. You stay in your room. You don't want to party. You poke at your food. We've all noticed. Something's not right."

Zeke was many things, but stupid wasn't one of them. I wasn't sure I could lie to him and him not call me out on it. He had a blunt nature and no room for bullshit. Those were two of the biggest reasons I respected him so much.

I could trust him, but still, I didn't want anyone knowing about my situation. I didn't want the guys running around feeling sorry for me or trying to talk me into treatments that would make me feel even worse than I already did.

So I did what I always did in a serious moment.

I laughed.

"What the hell, man? You, too! You boys are something else." I chuckled.

Zeke didn't laugh with me. He didn't even smile. Instead, he crossed his arms over his chest and waited silently—brooding in his usual way—telling me with his eyes that he knew I was full of shit.

I sobered and squeezed the back of my neck. "I'm fine, Zeke. No bullshit."

"No bullshit?" He shook his head. "I call bullshit on your no bullshit."

He moved closer so the crew members packing up couldn't hear him.

"We'll figure it out at some point, Chet. Whatever it is, we're here, bro. We'll always be here." He reached out and squeezed my shoulder.

He moved around me and started toward the exit. Before he stepped through the door, he turned back around.

"Also, if you want a burger, come get it yourself. I'm not your fucking bitch."

And then he was gone, leaving me laughing at his final words.

I fucking loved my bandmates ... my brothers.

My headache turned into something much worse, and I found myself gripping at my hair in my bunk, silently tortured as the bus swayed to our next destination. I hadn't enjoyed even a second of New Orleans, and I was glad to be moving on.

My painkillers were running low, and I wasn't sure how long it would take to get more, so I tried to keep my doses small. I took just enough to keep me from passing out from the pain.

I felt guilty carrying around narcotics since Tiny had some issues with addiction. It had gotten bad during the Rock Across America tour ... so bad that Constance almost died from an overdose. Because of that, I kept my stash tucked away and made sure to never be caught taking my pills in front of the guys.

Tears worked themselves from my eyes and crept down my face before rolling over the freshly shaved sides of my head. I wasn't much for crying. I'd only done it a handful of times in my life, but the pain was ridiculous. It was like a vise clamping my brain, squeezing so tightly and throbbing so hard that I couldn't think straight.

I didn't have much longer. I was sure of it. Death was nipping at my ass, and I wasn't sure I could hold him off much longer. I wasn't sure I wanted to. The symptoms were getting worse—the pain was unbearable. It wasn't until the ache and pressure grew so bad, and I finally passed out, that I got even a tiny bit of rest.

I woke up in Florida. The bus was empty, and when I climbed from my bunk, I could see the heat rising from the asphalt outside the bus in blurry waves. My pounding headache had waned a bit, but the pressure remained. Reaching into my bunk, I snatched my bottle of pain pills and downed two of them as quickly as I could.

I couldn't go on like this much longer. There was no need to suffer for the last few weeks of my life. I couldn't do it. I wouldn't. So once our next show was over, I was hauling ass back to California on a plane to see my doctor. I could make it back in time for the next show, but if I didn't get something more for the pain, I wouldn't be very good for the guys on stage anyway.

After tossing on some clothes, I stepped off the bus and into the Florida humidity. Even behind my shades, my eyes hurt from the brightness, which of course, added to the aggravating ache in my brain.

Shutting the bus door behind me, I strutted across the parking zone to the back of the venue we would be playing that night. A few crew members scurried around, rushing to finish putting together the set. Usually, I spoke with them and shot the shit for a few, but today, I couldn't bring myself to talk. It hurt too much. Every fucking thing hurt too much.

Thank fuck the venue had its air-conditioning on full blast because, by the time I stepped foot into the dim hallway, I was about to pass out from the excruciating heat mixing with the sledgehammer that was beating its way through my head.

I kept walking until I heard Zeke's guitar. He was tuning, and bits of the song kept playing and stopping. The closer I got, the louder the music became. The louder the music became, the worse my head pounded. Until finally, the pain became too much, and the space around me began to spin.

Stopping, I placed a hand against the wall to anchor myself. I just needed to make it through that night's show. After that, I could haul ass and get relief. Fourteen songs ... I could play fourteen songs.

I moved again, and again, the room spun. I felt like a little bitch with the vapors or some shit. Being sick didn't work for me. Losing control didn't work for me either, which was precisely what was happening. I was losing control.

My forehead was sweaty and stuck to the wall when I pressed my head against it. The pounding was getting harder and the pain worse. I gripped at the strands of hair falling into my eyes, pulling for relief that never came, and then I heard her voice break through the chaotic sounds of my own blood as it rushed through my diseased brain.

Hope.

Her name held so much meaning. Hope had given me some of the best nights of my life. And I was trying to hold on to hope that I'd stay alive for a few more months for my boys ... for my family. Either way, a little hope was all I needed ... her and the imaginary wish to survive.

"Are you okay, Chet?"

It was a simple question ... one that I would have usually answered with a lie pretty easily any other time, but not this time. Not when I felt like a knife was being shoved in the side of my brain.

I shook my head, finally opening up about something I'd kept secret for so long.

No.

I wasn't okay.

I would never be okay again.

Her hand warmed my arm, and I closed my eyes against the pleasure of having her touch me so innocently.

I'd been touched by women a lot since I was thirteen years old, but none of them even compared to Hope's touch. The way she made me feel, even while being a bitch, was intoxicating. Sadly, I couldn't even enjoy the feeling with my head hurting as badly as it was.

"Here"—she guided me across the hallway to a row of chairs—"have a seat. Do you need me to get someone for you?"

My knees shook as I sat down, and when she tried to pull away from me, I latched on to her hand and held it against my skin.

"No."

I didn't like that she was seeing me in such a weak position. I didn't want anyone else to see me this way.

"What's going on with you, Chet?"

Finally, I looked up. My eyes raked across her ivory skin, taking in a few of her tattoos, her slender shoulders, and her long neck, before landing on her face.

She was beautiful. Most women were, but Hope held a different kind of beauty. It was silent and humble. She tried to hide it behind thickly lined eyes and tattoos, but it was clear as day on her flushed cheeks and in her fathomless dark eyes.

"I just drank too much last night," I lied without blinking.

I could see in her expression that she didn't believe me, but I continued anyway.

"I need to lay off the mixed drinks and nose candy," I joked.

She didn't smile. Instead, she shook her head.

"You have a problem, Chet. You should tell someone before it's too late," she said, standing and pulling her hand away from my arm.

"I do," I agreed. "I need to lay off the drugs and drinking."

Again, she shook her head. "That's not the problem I'm talking about, and you damn well know it. You shouldn't lie so much, Chet."

I chuckled at the irony of her words.

She was calling me a liar when she'd laid the biggest lie ever on me a few nights before.

124

Fuck that.

"You should take your own advice," I snapped.

Between her pushing and my pulse beating in my brain, I couldn't continue to be the nice guy.

"Excuse me?"

"I said," I growled. "You should take your own advice. You should stop lying, too."

Her hands flew to her hips as her leg kicked out to the side with attitude. "And what the fuck did I lie about?" she asked.

I saw the moment realization filled her eyes, but it was too late; she had already asked the question.

I stood on shaking knees and pulled my shades from my face to look her in the eye.

"You lied about using me. You lied about the reason you left. You're a liar, Hope."

She didn't respond.

Instead, she turned and walked away, leaving me with an aching head and a stomach full of guilt.

I moved to follow her, but again, the hallway spun.

It wasn't going to work. I couldn't even stand straight, much less play a set with the guys, but I had to push through. The show must go on, and so must I.

17

HOPE

I got away from Chet as fast as I could. Even though he was obviously in distress about something, I couldn't remain in such a small space alone with him.

This was the number one rule I gave myself.

Stay the fuck away from Chet.

He smelled so good. Whatever cologne he was wearing was making my mouth water. And his sleeveless shirt showed off all his sexy as fuck tattoos. But none of that mattered. All that mattered was that I get away from him.

No thinking about how great he smelled.

No thinking about how great he felt.

None of that.

So I left him in the hallway and went to the stage so we could finish setup for that night's show. I felt terrible leaving him, but he kept pushing my buttons. He kept calling me out on my lie, which made me uncomfortable.

He wasn't lost like he was last time, but he was pale and sweaty. I wasn't sure how serious he was about the whole drinking and drugs thing, but something was definitely going on with Chet. Part of me wanted to go to the guys and tell them—maybe drop a little birdie in Constance's ear—but at the same time, I knew it was none of my fucking business.

So I kept it to myself and went to work.

That night, before it was even time for the boys to go on stage, there was a knock on our bus door. Constance opened it to find Tiny, Finn, and Zeke staring back at her.

"What's up? Aren't you guys about to go on?" she asked.

"We can't find Chet." I heard Tiny say.

My heart squeezed in my chest.

I shouldn't care if he was okay, but I did.

"What do you mean you can't find Chet?" Lena asked as she pushed around Constance.

The guys joined us on our bus, taking up a ton of space and making the bus feel three times smaller.

"When's the last time you saw him?" I asked.

I should have stayed out of it. I really should have, but I couldn't help myself.

"Last night on the bus," Zeke answered.

That couldn't be right. I'd seen Chet earlier in the hallway just outside setup. He looked as though he was headed to tune and set up.

"But I saw him in the hallway earlier today," I blurted, instantly wishing I hadn't included myself in their conversation. "He didn't show up for prep?"

Finn shook his head. "Nope, and when I see him again, if he's okay, I'm going to kick his ass."

I was on the verge of telling the guys what I'd seen earlier and about the incident in Vegas when Chet was entirely out of it. I was on the verge of telling them all about finding Chet lost in the hallway of our hotel, and about seeing him in the hallway earlier when he was pale and sweaty. But when I opened my mouth to talk, a loud thump sounded on the bus door.

"That's him," Finn said, going to the door and opening it.

Chet climbed on board. He looked ready to go on stage in his ripped jeans and black shirt. He was ready for the show with a radiant smile plastered across his face while he twirled his sticks between his fingers.

127

"What's going on? We gonna play or what?" he asked as if nothing was going on.

"Damn." He whistled. "Y'all got the hookup," he said as he took in our bus and the nice setup.

"Where the fuck have you been all day?" Finn asked, stepping forward. "We were worried and shit, man."

Zeke shook his head and sighed. "I told you something was up, but nobody fucking listens to me."

"I'm fine. Everything's fine," Chet said, throwing his arms out in aggravation. "I just went and bullshitted around Tallahassee, but I'm back now, and I'm ready to play this set. So let's go, bitches."

He didn't even look my way before he turned and left our bus. The guys grumbled a bit before turning and following.

Something was up. Even the guys were talking about it. But still, I would keep to my own business and let the chips fall where they may when it came to Chet and his problems.

His problems.

Not mine.

Before our show, I'd gone out and listened on the side stage as the boys played. Every now and again, Chet would look my way, but I pretended to be watching Finn. He didn't need to know I was checking him out throughout the show. He didn't need to know that I could barely keep my eyes off his naked, tattooed chest.

Chet had a habit of stripping throughout the show. I understood. I knew how hot it got under the lights of the stage, but Chet took it to the extreme. He'd start out fully dressed, and sometimes end the show in his boxers.

It was one of those nights, and he looked amazing sweaty and glistening beneath the stage lights as he focused and put his all into playing his drums. I wanted to step on stage and move closer to him. I wanted to feel the pounding of his kick drum and the vibration of his strikes.

Somehow, I managed to stay put. Even as my body ached for the things he could do to it. I'd gone cold turkey when it came to Chet, but that didn't mean I wasn't craving just one more hit of him.

The girls soon joined me, and we sang along from the side of the stage. Every now and again, Tiny would step over to the side and pull Constance onto the stage for a kiss, making the crowd go wild. It was a good time, and it wasn't long before the boys were finishing, and Finn was announcing us.

I'd never get used to the crowd's screams when we stepped on stage. Hearing people call our names and watching them mouth our songs back to us from the front row was amazing. I rarely got to see it since I was usually parked at my set on the back of the stage, but thanks to the big screens placed around the venue, I'd get a look at them close up on occasion.

We played a sold-out show, and the crowd was wild, just the way we liked them. By the time we made it to the stage, the guys had the crowd warmed up, and most of them were fucked up out of their minds.

Men jumped on the stage to get to one of us. One even made it to Lena to kiss her on the cheek before the crew yanked him from the stage. Sometimes, it was scary, but we knew the staff had our backs.

By the time our show was over, I was drenched in sweat and full of so much fucking energy I thought I'd pop. After playing an encore of our biggest hit, we ran off the stage and went straight to our bus. A crowd waited outside the venue for us, and the crew members had to block us as we ran through the hordes of screaming fans.

It was so unreal that my life had changed so much. It was unreal that people were screaming for us and wanting something ... anything signed. It was a thing of beauty. Something I'd cherish for always.

I was in the back, running after the girls, when suddenly, a wall of heat blocked my path. I ran into a sweaty chest, and his scent was more disturbing than the red food stains plastered across his white T-shirt.

I pulled back, my eyes moving up the tall wall blocking my path, and my eyes clashed with a strange man staring down at me. His hands locked around the tops of my arms, and before I could stop him, his mouth came down on mine. I pulled back, my lips remaining sealed as I struggled in his hold, and once I was free, I didn't hold back. Rearing back with my right arm, I gave him everything I had as I caught him in the nose with my fist.

His hands cupped his nose, and blood squeezed between his fingers and dripped onto his stained shirt.

"You bitch!" he muffled through his hands.

I moved to hit him again, but before I could, someone lifted me and tossed me over their shoulder.

"Let me go!" I screamed.

I fought in their hold, struggling to get away until I noticed whoever was holding me was taking me to the bus. The girls appeared behind me with grins on their faces as I continued to cuss the person manhandling me.

"You got him so fucking good, Hope," Lena said with a chuckle.

"Beware of the right hook." Twiggy laughed.

They thought the shit was funny. Meanwhile, I was still raring for more.

I squirmed against a muscled arm and clawed at the back of the person carrying me.

"Keep it up, Blackbird." Chet chuckled, smacking me on the ass. "That shit's turning me on."

Instantly, I stopped clawing and fighting and went limp in his hold.

We cleared the crowd, and I could hear the hum of the waiting buses and smell the burn of their diesel. Chet could have put me down since I was calm again and back in safe territory, but he didn't. Instead, he continued to carry me until we were at the door to the Siren's bus.

I narrowed my eyes at him the second he set me on my feet. The girls climbed the stairs onto the bus, leaving me behind with only Chet.

I panicked.

"First of all, I had that situation under control," I said.

He shook his head. "Sure, you did."

I ignored his sarcastic response and continued.

"Secondly, don't ever call me Blackbird again," I seethed. He didn't flinch.

Instead, he stared down at me unmoving, his eyes moving over my face as if he was searching me for something.

"I like the name," he said. "It reminds me."

I knew what he was talking about. I knew what he was being reminded of … our night together. But I didn't want to remember. I was already having issues trying to forget.

"Remind you of what?" I snapped. "There's never been anything, and there'll never be anything to be reminded of."

His eyes narrowed as he moved closer, pinning me against the side of the bus.

"I'm getting about sick of your fucking attitude, Blackbird." He reached up and smoothed a strand of my hair between two fingers.

I smacked his hand away and turned my head to the side so our faces weren't so close.

"I suggest you get used to it. The more you fuck with me, the more attitude you will get."

He moved even closer, his body pressing into mine, making me thankful it was dark out, and no one could see us. His fingers dug into my cheeks, making them ache, and I dug my nails into his hand, trying to pull it away.

"Keep opening your mouth, and I'll stick something in it," he threatened.

"I dare you, motherfucker. I'll bite your cock off, and you know I will."

And I would.

Either that, or I'd lose myself completely and suck the flavor from his stick. He didn't need to know how badly I wanted to taste him, though. If anything, his roughness and the way he was manhandling me was turning me on.

In the red glow of the parking lights of the buses around us, I saw his eyes shift from mine to my lips.

"I've never been afraid of a little nibble."

I laughed sarcastically, tugging at his hand as I tried to free my face from his grasp.

"I don't nibble. I bite."

Again, his eyes moved over my face, and his fingers loosened their hold.

"I want to fuck you."

His change in demeanor left me spinning. I knew Chet, and I understood his being rough was his form of foreplay. It was mine, too, but his switch in mood was so fast it caught me off guard.

"No."

I said the word, but my body rebelled, sending an electric shot to my cunt. I grew wet for him, even as I narrowed my eyes at him and tried to move away from his hold.

"It's going to happen, Hope. You might as well give in."

He didn't know what he was talking about because I wouldn't let it happen. No matter how much I wanted to feel him. No matter how much he pushed against me and promised to wreck my body. I wouldn't give in. I couldn't.

I tugged weakly, my body trying to stay while my mind begged to leave, but he wrapped his arms around me and pulled me closer.

"First, I'm going to eat your pussy. I'll suck your sweet cunt until you scream and fill my mouth." I closed my eyes, my body getting wetter with each word. My clit throbbed, begging for any sort of attention. "Then I'm going to stick my cock inside you. I'm going to fuck you so hard you come apart."

He pressed his forehead to mine, his hot breath striking my lips with each of his pants.

"When I close my eyes, I can still feel your tight pussy wrapped around me. It's hot and wet, squeezing me so hard until I come deep inside you." He trembled. "You want me, Hope. You want to fuck me. Your body knows it. I can tell by the chills covering your skin. I can smell your wet heat. You know where to find me when you get your mind on board."

Then he released me and walked away without looking back.

My knees shook from his words, my slit throbbing so hard for his intrusion I had to press my back against the bus to hold me up.

His whispered words moved over my body like a hot wave. My nipples grew harder, almost pained in their desire.

I couldn't get on the bus like this. The girls would take one look at me and know. As it was, I'm sure they heard us arguing just outside the bus. Chet and I rarely talked to each other. They would have questions. They would want to know what was going on.

It was the last thing I wanted.

Still, we had to pull out soon and head to our next gig, which meant I didn't have any choice. Pulling myself from the cool, metal side of the bus, I pulled open the door and climbed on board.

Thankfully, the girls said nothing. They didn't even look my way as I walked through the bus toward my bunk. I didn't have any answers for them. I didn't really have any for myself. The only thing I knew was the second the girls were asleep, and I had some alone time, I was touching myself.

I'd come quietly in my bunk while secretly thinking about all the delicious things he promised.

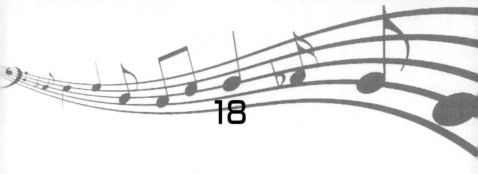

18

CHET

We pulled out for the four-hour drive to Orlando right after the Siren's show. I left Hope outside her bus with a raging hard-on and the hammer destroying my brain. The boys played video games and talked to their wives for the ride, but I lay in my bunk in agony.

We were playing four different shows in the Orlando area, which meant we would be hotel living for a few days. Usually, I'd be pumped about the amusements parks. I was a child at heart, and being that close to Disney World with the money to go was awesome, but I couldn't think about any of that.

I checked into my room like usual, leaving the guys to go to their rooms, and went straight to my shower. I'd already booked my flight to California, and I had three hours until I was leaving. I didn't even unpack. Instead, I left my things on the bed, only taking what I needed for the quick trip back to California, and left as soon as I was showered and dressed.

Our first Orlando show was the following night, which meant I was cutting it super close, but I had to do what I had to do. I'd make it back in time for my boys. It would be a lot, and I'd be fucking exhausted by the time I stepped on stage, but I knew I could pull it off.

The guys were aggravated with me, and I didn't blame them. I'd been so fucked up on tour. I was all over the place. I barely hung out with the guys, and I was sure my distance was noticeable, but I had to do it. I was a fucking mess, and things were getting worse. If I didn't get back to Doctor Patel soon, I wouldn't make it through the rest of the tour.

I took a cab to the airport, feeling like shit for leaving the guys without telling them, but one of the best things about being me was that nothing was unexpected. The guys trusted me. They knew I'd be there when it was time to step on stage. This wasn't the first time I'd disappeared on them, and it probably wouldn't be the last. They would bitch when it was time to go on, but they were used to it.

The non-stop flight from Orlando to Los Angeles was six hours. I called Doctor Patel on his personal phone once I was settled into a cab and on the way to his office. He knew I was coming, and thanks to my rock star status, he pulled strings for me.

I got to his office two hours later. It was after hours, so the office was dark and empty. The fake plants that lined the waiting room looked like jagged shadows. I'd never been inside a dark, empty doctor's office. It was creepy.

Doctor Patel met me at the front door. He was wearing jeans and a button-up instead of his usual long white lab coat. He didn't look like a doctor; he looked like a man about to hang with his friends.

I followed him to his office, and once he settled behind his desk, he finally looked at me.

"You look like shit," he said.

Doctor Patel wasn't your typical doctor, and we'd grown past our doctor/patient relationship over time. He no longer doctored me. Instead, he was blunt and to the point, exactly how I liked it. It was one of the main reasons I always ran back to him.

"I feel like shit."

"What's going on?"

"The headaches are getting worse, and sometimes, I lose track of what I'm doing. I forget where I am or who I am. It doesn't last long, but it's scary as fuck."

He shook his head and tapped the edge of his desk. "You need to have the surgery, Chet. This tumor isn't going to just go away. If your symptoms are getting worse, then it's probably growing."

"I can't."

When Doctor Patel had first mentioned surgery, I was all for it. I wasn't afraid to be put under. Let them chop at my brain if it meant waking up and being normal again, but that wasn't the case. It wasn't until he started talking about what could go wrong that I pulled back.

A forty-five percent chance I could wake up blind was terrible, but it was the fifty percent chance I'd never pick up a drumstick again that was the big fuck no. A fifty percent chance was too great a risk in my book. I couldn't live without my eyes and my ability to play drums. Drums were my life. So instead of having the surgery, I was determined to live was what left of my life to the fullest.

"You can do this, Chet. The surgery has its risks, but you can't live like this, man. High on pain pills until the end. That's no way to live."

"Yeah, but it's better than being blind. It's better than never playing again."

He sighed.

"You're sure this is what you want?"

I nodded. "I'm sure a life without my drums isn't much of a life for me."

"There's a fifty percent chance that things could go wrong, but there's also a fifty percent chance that you could wake up and things would be fine. You'd be you again, Chet. Isn't that what you want?"

"I'm sorry. I can't take that chance."

And I couldn't.

I wouldn't.

The risks were too high. I'd rather die than live my life dependent on people because I couldn't see. Thanks to my tumor, I'd gone blind before. And although it was brief, it was terrible. I could never do it permanently.

The blindness was scary, but I wouldn't know what to do with myself if I couldn't play. It was a punishment worse than death as far as I was concerned. The tumor's location promised all kinds of problems, but I could still play right now. If by some chance, the tumor continued to grow and that ability was taken away from me, I'd consider the surgery. Until then, it was a big fuck no.

Doctor Patel stood and chuckled softly to himself. "Then let's get you an MRI and take a peek and see how much it's grown. I'll see what I can do for pain management."

The tumor had definitely grown, but on top of that tumor, there was a new one. It was small, pressing against essential blood vessels and threatening my occipital areas.

In other words, I was fucked.

"Another fucking tumor?" I laughed. "That's just my luck."

I could laugh about my situation now. I'd gone through it all, and the fact that I'd lived as long as I had was a miracle in itself ... especially considering how I'd lived.

Drugs.

Sex.

Rock 'n' roll.

The works.

I lived balls to the wall and balls deep every fucking day. Or at least I had before my brain started to feel like it would explode.

No.

I'd lived that way until Hope, but I wouldn't admit that aloud.

Living on the edge was the least I could do, considering. You know, the whole going out with a bang shit.

That was me.

Living on the edge.

Always.

Then again, maybe it was because I was living so hard that I was still alive. A body at rest went into rest mode, and there was no rest for the wicked fucks like me. Always on the go. New pussy every other night. Shit. I was living the life of a fucking king.

Until Hope.

Not that I was blaming her that things were catching up with me, but obviously, slowing down wasn't the way to go, and being with Hope made me secretly want to slow down.

All my boys were settled down, living the domesticated life, but not me. Hell, no. Anchoring a woman to me would be cruel, and while I was known to stick my cock in something new every other day in the past, I wasn't a cruel man. I couldn't do that to Hope, if she even wanted me that way.

"I'm going to say you have six months." Doctor Patel's words broke through my thoughts, making the air rush from my body.

He was also smiling. He knew there was no need to pull the standard sad doctor bullshit talks with me. I was dying a motherfucker, and we both knew it. I kept coming back to him because he kept shit real. No sugarcoating, and I was all for that.

I knew I was on borrowed time, but I'd never had a date set in mind. I just went about my days, wondering if I had months, weeks, or days. I thought knowing would make me feel better.

It didn't.

Six months wasn't a long time, but I'd make the best of it for as long as possible.

"Okay. I got some serious partying to get under my belt." I chuckled, patting my knees as I stood.

"Try to keep the drugs and drinking to a minimum. I don't want you taking anyone else down with you."

"Ah, come on now, doc. You know I'm going down in a blaze of glory. Fuck minimum."

Doctor Patel laughed out loud, shaking his head. He knew me well since I'd been his patient for over two years. He repeatedly tried to get me to have the surgery and all the other shit that would make my life hell, but I wasn't having it.

Fuck that.

If God wanted me, he wasn't going to have much of a fight on his hands. And since I knew I had to go, I would live loud and hard until I took my last breath.

Three hours later, I headed back to the airport in another cab. I lay back against the seat and replayed Doctor Patel's words with closed eyes.

He switched me to another painkiller and sent me on my way with a promise that I'd come back to him and consider the surgery if it got worse. I promised, even though I knew that wouldn't happen. I had no reason to live. Not really. But I had plenty of reasons to see and play.

One thing was for sure, I had to stay away from Hope ... my Blackbird. I'd denied it to myself for a while now, but I was starting to feel things for her, and I wasn't willing to let that happen. It wasn't fair to her or me to start bringing emotions into something that could never be. Plus, I wasn't so sure she wanted anything more to do with me anyway.

I'd get my ass back to Florida, play the fuck out of my drums, and even though I know I shouldn't, I'd spend at least one more night inside Hope. I had everything else I could want in life; she was the one thing missing. I'd enjoy her once more before I let her go. It was the humane thing to do instead of dragging her along with my crazy bullshit. She would go back to hating me. She'd probably stop talking to me, but it was what I had to do. Either way, things weren't going to end well for her when it came to me.

I checked my phone for the time as the cab pulled up to the airport, but it was dead. I hadn't thought to bring my charger, and since I depended on my phone for everything, including my contact list, I had no idea what anyone's number was.

It didn't matter. The clock inside the airport told me I was going to make it. Hell, at this rate, the guys wouldn't have even noticed I was missing ... hopefully.

It wasn't until I saw that my flight had been delayed that I started to freak out. I'd make it back in time to play if it was the last thing I did, but if that didn't happen by some chance, I knew the shit would hit the fan. The guys were going to be so pissed. Not showing up wasn't an option, but the longer I sat in the airport, the more it looked like I wouldn't make it back in time.

19

Hope

"C het's not here," Constance said as she burst into the room.

"What? What do you mean he's not here?" Lena asked.

"They go on in twenty minutes," Mia said as she stood from the couch.

We were relaxing in the back of the venue in a dressing room. We usually watched the boys play a few minutes before they started. But it didn't seem like that was going to happen.

"Where is he?" I asked.

Constance turned my way, her eyes wide with worry.

"They don't know. They went to his room this afternoon, but he wasn't there. All his shit's on his bed, but he's gone."

He hadn't shown up for breakfast, but the guys hadn't been too worried. Chet was famous for sleeping the morning away after a long night, but he would never miss a show. Something was definitely wrong.

"What are they going to do?" I asked.

As soon as the words left my lips, the boys entered our space. Their worry was evident in their stiff shoulders and tight lips.

"Tell me you know our songs, Hope," Finn said as he fell onto the couch next to me.

My eyes moved around the room, landing on each of the guys looking back at me. "You're serious?"

Finn nodded. "We don't know where he is. He's probably fucked up with some girl, but thousands of fans are waiting for us. We'll deal with Chet later, but until then, can you cover for him?"

I nodded, my heart beating so hard with anxiety that I was starting to feel sick.

I knew Blow Hole's songs. I'd played their songs for fun many times, but walking on stage and playing in front of thousands of fans was a different story. Our music was engraved in my brain, coming out without even thinking, but Blow Hole's songs weren't.

What if I fucked up?

What if I missed a beat?

As if hearing my thoughts, Finn reached out and placed a hand on my shoulder. "You'll do great, Hope. You'd be saving our asses, and we'd be eternally grateful."

I nodded, feeling my heart lodged in my throat. "I'll do it."

At least, I'd try. I didn't want to let the guys down. They'd already been let down by Chet.

I paced the dressing room for a few, trying to calm my nerves. And then, ten minutes later, I stepped onto the stage with the Blow Hole boys. It was a true honor to play with the boys. I could remember going to The Pit before anyone knew who they were and watching and wishing I could step on stage with them.

I was living the dream. As I sat in front of Chet's set, my eyes bounced over the drums. Skulls decorated the outer edges, and his name was etched into the silver trim. The set was expensive and nicer than mine, but I still longed to play my own.

I zoned out while Finn tossed out a lie to explain Chet's absence and introduced me. I stood and held my drumsticks over my head when the crowd grew louder for me. My heart slammed into my ribs, making my breathing hard and shallow. Dizziness swooped in, but I pushed through my nerves and slammed the drumsticks against the drums.

I played harder for the boys than I ever did for the Sirens. Not because they mattered more, but because I was so fucking worried I'd screw something up. I knew what I was doing when it came to playing with my girls, but while I knew Blow Hole's music well, some songs, I'd never played before.

I hadn't been nervous on the stage since my first time playing in front of people, but I made it through. And when the boys said their goodnights, I smiled, knowing I'd kicked way more ass than I knew I was capable of.

I left the stage with the boys, wiped at the sweat pouring down my back, and then I went right back on with my girls. I was exhausted; my arms ached from playing so hard, and my back was stiff, but I'd played double shows before.

Our songs were in my memory, which meant I played in a more relaxed state. Halfway through our show, I stripped off my T-shirt, leaving only my sports bra. A breeze hit the stage every few minutes, sending chills across my arms, but the second I realized Chet was standing on the side stage watching me play, the chills spread down my back and up my neck.

My eyes skimmed him once, but I refused to look at him anymore. I was pissed at him. One, for leaving his group hanging while he was probably out fucking some bitch, and two, because he was probably out fucking some bitch.

I didn't have the right to be jealous, but I was. I knew what it meant to love the drums. I knew what it meant to love my group. And I also knew Chet felt the same way about playing the drums and Blow Hole. Whoever took up his time and made him miss a show must have been pretty special.

Those thoughts made me sick to my stomach, and I accidentally skipped a beat, making Lena turn my way in confusion. I nodded that I was okay and kept playing, blocking out anything involving Chet and the bullshit feelings I had for him.

20

CHET

I tossed more than enough money to the cab driver and ran inside the venue as fast as I could. I knew I was too late, but I couldn't help but continue to rush. I felt like shit; guilt had eaten me alive on the flight back to Florida. I'd never left my boys hanging before, and I wasn't sure how they would handle it. I just knew I wasn't taking it well.

The crew members ushered me into the back of the venue, screaming into their walkies that I'd been located. As I entered the sounding area, the Siren's music echoed all around me. I'd missed our entire set. I'd really missed it. I could hardly believe I'd done something so careless.

I searched the venue for the boys, but they were nowhere to be found. Obviously, the show had gone on, and I could only assume that Hope had taken my place behind my drums. If there were anyone I'd want to take my place behind my set, it would be her. Although, I hated that my boys were put in a fucked-up predicament because of me.

I went to the side stage and watched the girls play. Hope turned her eyes on me briefly before turning away. Either she didn't see me, or she was seriously pissed off. The way her face turned red and her shoulders stiffened, she was seriously pissed off.

I didn't blame her.

I watched for two songs, gathering my thoughts and figuring out what to tell the guys before leaving for the hotel. I went to Finn's room first. I had no fucking idea what I was going to tell him, but I had to make it right. With my life on borrowed time, I didn't want any bad blood between my boys and me.

I tapped at his door, and within seconds, the door swung open, and he, Zeke, and Tiny were standing there staring back at me. I opened my mouth to speak, but before I could, Finn pulled me into a bear hug. His large arms squeezed around me, and my guilt increased. I felt sick to my stomach with regret and sadness.

"Where the fuck have you been, Chet?" Zeke asked.

He didn't sound angry. If anything, he sounded relieved.

I pulled back from Finn and looked up at him. There was definitely relief in his expression.

"I'm sorry, guys," I said. "I'm so fucking sorry."

Tiny grabbed my shoulder and squeezed with a firm hand. "Fuck it, man. You're here, and you're alive. That's all that matters."

"Yeah," Finn agreed. "We called you so many times. I didn't know if you were dead on the side of the fucking street somewhere."

"You should have at least called, Chet," Zeke followed.

I reached into my pocket and pulled out my dead phone.

"It's dead. I don't know any of your numbers. I tried to get back here. I tried so hard, but my fucking flight got delayed, and ...."

I stopped when I realized what I'd said.

How could I slip up so easily?

"Your flight? Where the fuck did you go, Chet?" Finn asked.

His voice was tinted with anger, and I knew now that the guys knew I was alive and well, their anger would come out. I was okay with that. I deserved their rage.

"It's no big deal," I started. "I went back to the condo real quick to check on things. I had plenty of time to get back, but the damn flight was delayed."

It was a lie. A stupid one at that, but I said the first thing that came to mind.

Finn's brows lifted. Obviously, he didn't believe a word I was saying.

"You went home to check on the condo? For what?"

"I just went to get away and make sure everything was locked down and okay." I shrugged.

"You're lying," Zeke yelled and moved toward me, prompting Finn to grab his arm. Zeke stopped and looked up at Finn. "What? He's lying. He's been lying about something since this fucking tour started."

He turned away, sitting on Finn's bed and shaking his head.

"I don't know what your problem is, Chet, but whatever it is, you need to fix it. Finn and Tiny have seen it, too. Something's up, and if you can't at least tell us what it is, then what kind of friends are we, man?"

"He's right, man," Tiny muttered. "You've been fucked up since we left California."

I was tired of the lies.

Tired of the bullshit.

I couldn't keep up with it anymore. I was an honest man. I always had been. Even with the women I'd fucked over the years, I'd always been brutally honest about my intentions, and this dishonesty was killing me.

I tugged at my hair, aggravation and the events of the past few months coming to a head. Everything moved over me, and I found myself breaking down. My headache, which I'd soothed over with a double dose of morphine, was returning, slamming into my brain and making me flinch.

"I can't fucking do this right now," I said, spinning around and leaving the guys staring back at me. "It's too much."

I moved toward the door, prepared to leave and hoping they forgot about my missed show and we could move on.

"Leave, Chet," Finn called out, stopping me in my tracks.

"Excuse me?"

"If you're not here with us one hundred percent, you should head back to California. We can hire a replacement drummer for the rest of the tour. Thankfully, Hope knew our music tonight."

"You want me to leave?"

I could hardly believe Finn was saying these things to me. We were boys ... brothers. Hell, I'd lived with Finn growing up. We were there for each other ... always had been. They said they had my back. They'd always had my back.

"I thought we stuck together?" I asked, swallowing against the hurt in my chest.

"We do, man." His voice softened. "But you obviously have some serious shit going on. We can't afford to have you freak out and leave us in the middle of the tour again. Whatever it is, go home and deal with it. We'll finish the tour."

"No," I said adamantly. "This is my group too. This band is my life. It's the only thing holding my shit together. I'll be there. I won't miss another fucking show. I'm not going anywhere. I'm not leaving y'all in the middle of a fucking tour."

Zeke stood and crossed his arms. Tiny joined him. All three stared back at me like they didn't believe me, and I hated that I'd somehow become untrustworthy with my boys. I'd never do anything on purpose to jeopardize everything we worked for. They had to know that.

Finally, Finn nodded.

"Go get some rest, man. We'll grab breakfast in the morning and get ready for tomorrow night's show. This isn't over. Not by a long shot. When we get home, we sit and talk this shit out. Got it?"

I nodded, agreeing that by then, I'd be more than willing to let them know what was going on. "Got it."

I left Finn's room feeling like shit. I hated that things were tense between us, and I was sure it would be obvious at tomorrow night's show, but right now wasn't the time.

I was tired. The guys were tired. We could start over fresh tomorrow, and once we were home and settled, I'd tell them.

My original plan didn't include telling them, but things were different now. The reality was rapidly crashing over me. Things weren't going as planned ... nothing ever did, but I'd go with the flow the way I always did. And when it was all over and done with, I'd tell the boys, and I'd die peacefully without any regrets.

My room door was in front of me, and I knew I should have stepped in, showered, and gone to sleep, but I couldn't. After the news I got from Doctor Patel, my room was the last place I wanted to be. All I could think about was going to Hope. Being near her always made me feel better ... lighter, like the weight of the world wasn't on my shoulders.

My feet moved on their own, their destination sure, and I found myself standing outside Hope's room.

Just one more time.

I just wanted to be with her once more.

Then I'd leave her alone and never fuck with her again. After so many years of thinking of my Blackbird, of dreaming about being with her again and finding that solace in her arms, I couldn't just let her go. I'd found my Blackbird again ... I'd found Hope. I was a dying man, and she was my dying wish.

I deserved her at least once more. Well, maybe not deserved. I'd done some fucked-up shit in my time, but my days on Earth were numbered. If I were going to die, which I knew I was, one more time would have to be enough to last the rest of my lifetime.

I tapped on her door. Part of me wished she wouldn't be there. Obviously, I was weak when it came to her. Obviously, I couldn't control myself. If she wasn't there, then I could walk away, get a shower, and go to bed. If she wasn't there, I'd be off the hook for the night.

The door opened, and she stood there in only her T-shirt and shorts. She looked delicious ... the perfect last meal for a

148

dying man. The second my eyes landed on her, I knew I had to have her. I had to taste her.

"No," she blurted before she shut the door in my face.

I reached out and stopped it with the palm of my hand.

"Hope, just let me explain."

She pressed at the door, trying her hardest to shut me out, but I wasn't having it.

"I don't want to hear your lies, Chet. I can't be friends with someone who could leave their crew like sitting ducks. I don't even want to think about who you were fucking. It's disgusting."

And then I knew.

She was angry with me for leaving the boys hanging and putting her on the spot by having to play for me but hidden beneath her anger was jealousy. She thought I was out fucking some chick instead of showing up to the set.

"I wasn't fucking anyone, Hope. I swear it."

She stopped pressing at the door, allowing me to push it open until I could see her face again.

"I haven't touched anyone since you. That's the God's honest truth."

She crossed her arms over her braless chest and shrugged.

"I don't care who you fuck, but what you did to the guys was bullshit."

I stepped into her room, and she didn't try to stop me. Once I had the door shut behind me, I pulled her to me. She smelled shower fresh, like baby powder and shampoo. I loved the clean smell of her skin, and again, my mouth watered to taste her.

My lips had skimmed her soft neck before I sucked at the sweet skin.

"Don't lie, Blackbird; you care."

She shivered. "I don't," she whispered.

I nibbled at her neck, tugging the collar of her shirt out of my way until I could bite her slender shoulder.

"I'm sorry I put you on the spot. I'm sorry that you had to take the stage for me, but I promise I wasn't with another woman."

Usually, when a woman acted possessive, it was a major turn-off, but I liked Hope's jealousy. It made me feel powerful and made me forget about how sick and weak I was slowly becoming.

"Where were you?" she asked, leaning her head to the side and exposing more of her skin to me.

I took advantage, licking and sucking at her shoulders until I became annoyed with her shirt. My fingers had skimmed the hem of her shirt before I pulled it over her head.

She stood before me in only her shorts, and my eyes went to the tattoo that lived in my memories and symbolized one of the best nights of my life. Her skin was soft against my fingertips when I ran them across the inked bird. Chills broke out across her skin, and she sucked in a breath.

"I needed to take care of something," I answered.

It wasn't a lie, but it wasn't the complete truth. It was the least and most I could do for her at that moment.

"Why won't you tell me, Chet?"

I kissed the tattoo before moving down, letting my lips graze her skin.

"Tell you what?"

"Why won't you tell me what you're hiding?"

I chuckled against her body, my tongue peeking out to lick at a tiny freckle.

Without answering, I moved lower, sucking her hard nipple between my lips and making her body go tense in my arms. Her fingers tickled my hair as she pulled my face hard against her body.

The button of her shorts slipped through the buttonhole easily, and I was able to push them down over her hips. Thankfully, she wasn't wearing underwear, and I was able to touch her without any more barriers.

"Chet, we shouldn't."

Her words were weak and died away slowly when I slipped a finger into her wetness. She was always so wet and ready for me ... always so willing to let me please her. That was precisely what I'd do. Except for this time, it would be all for her. Don't get me wrong, tasting her was pleasurable for me, too, but there would be no fucking. Not tonight.

I moved her to the bed and began sucking her other nipple as I laid her back. Once she was flat, I took advantage ... moving lower and tasting every square inch of her. She squirmed beneath me, whispering things I couldn't understand as I slowly and leisurely licked, sucked, and kissed her beautiful body.

Once I reached her navel, her fingers were lost in my hair. She tugged, making my scalp sting and pushing me to please her.

Her thighs fell open for me, her swollen clit peeking from her wet folds and begging to be tasted. I tongued her slit, collecting her sweetness on my tongue and tasting everything she was. Her legs fell open, showing me how ready she was for me go to down on her.

My tongue twirled around her clit before I sucked at it, feeling it throb between my lips.

"Oh, my God," she whispered. "No, Chet, we can't."

I'd already started. There would be no stopping ... at least, not until she was coming in my mouth and screaming her release.

She was saying no, but her hand on my head pressed my mouth to her. I bit the inside of her thigh and chuckled.

"Your mouth says no, but your body says yes," I said.

Blowing softly on her wet flesh, I smiled when chills broke out across her skin.

"We shouldn't. It's ... it's wrong," she stuttered.

Grinning, I pressed a hot kiss against her throbbing pebble, and she sucked in a breath. "I know, baby, but doesn't it feel so fucking good?"

She moaned when I licked her again instead of answering my question.

"Answer me, Blackbird. Tell me how good it feels when I eat your pussy."

Her fingers tightened in my hair, pressing my face into her.

"So good," she mumbled. "Don't fucking stop."

So I didn't.

I licked, sucked, and tasted her until she exploded around my tongue, and I could taste the fresh sweetness of her climax.

I woke after a night full of hard, loud sex. Blackbird was my match in the bed, scratching at my skin and taking everything I could give without pulling away. She liked to be choked. She loved to ride my cock, and when it came to talking dirty, she was getting better and better every time we fucked.

She was warm and soft against my side, and her sleeping breaths whispered over my chest, sending a fresh wave of blood straight to my cock. Her leg was lying across my dick, and it pressed into the side of her bent knee as it hardened.

It was different with Hope. I didn't hate waking up with her, and I especially didn't hate how she felt snuggled against my side as she slept. A dim light filled the room from the rising sun outside the curtains, and I was able to see her face when I looked down at her.

She was so beautiful, even when she slept. Her face was soft in sleep; her lips parted slightly, letting her sleeping breaths rush in and out. Her dark lashes rested against her ivory skin, prompting me to reach out and touch her cheek.

And it was at that moment, as I caressed her cheek and smiled softly down at her, that it hit me.

I'd fallen for Hope.

Hard.

My body stiffened, my heart skipping a beat before slamming into my ribs in panic.

How did I let it happen?

I didn't know when it happened. It could have been five years ago when I became obsessed with Blackbird, for all I knew, but I was in love with Hope.

My chest tightened with my newfound knowledge, and my lungs squeezed, pushing the breath from my body and making it nearly impossible to inhale.

This couldn't happen.

I'd just found out the day before that I only had months to live.

How cruel was it that I'd finally fall in love with a woman only months before Death was set to take me?

I hadn't even noticed the crushing headache until then. I'd woken in total bliss in Hope's arms, not even realizing that my head was splitting. My eyes blurred with the pain, and I moved, sliding from her grasp and hoping I didn't wake her.

I wasn't ready to talk. I wasn't prepared to do anything but get my meds and take away the pain and hopefully the tightness in my chest, but the more I moved, the more she slowly began to wake.

"What's wrong?" she asked, her voice rough with sleep.

"I need to get going. I'm supposed to meet up with the guys for breakfast."

It wasn't a lie.

"Food," she growled against my chest before placing a soft kiss against my skin.

My heart sunk into my stomach, making me feel nauseated. The way she was treating me—the softness in her touch—was all too much. I needed to break this shit up. I needed to let her know fast that last night was the last time. There would never be anything more between us.

Just friends.

"Let me get a shower, and I'll go with you. I'm starving."

She climbed from the bed, her naked backside glowing in the dim sunlight spilling into the room.

I didn't want to hurt her ... I really didn't, but something told me she wouldn't care either way. She didn't care about me that way, even if her actions suggested she did. Hope was as hardcore as I was, and even though I'd accidentally developed feelings for her, I didn't think she'd be stupid enough to let that happen to her.

She was more intelligent ... more likely to protect herself against something as dangerous as a broken heart, but still, I had to cut this shit. I was a dying man. I had nothing to offer her, even if I wish I did ... even if I wanted more with her.

"I don't think that's a good idea," I said, hating myself for the shiver in my voice.

She stopped and turned to face me. Her body glowed in the morning light. Her nipples were hard from the cool air outside the blankets, her waist slim, and her thighs round with perfection. She was everything I could ever want, and everything I could never keep.

"What do you mean?"

"I don't know." I climbed from her bed and started to get dressed. "I think maybe we should go ahead and squash whatever this is."

I wasn't sure, but I think I heard her gasp at my words. I wasn't looking at her ... I couldn't. I was a coward, which meant I kept my head down as I pulled my shirt on.

"Whatever this is? What exactly is this?" she asked.

I could tell by the chill in her voice that she was getting angry. This wasn't going to end well.

"I mean, we're just two friends getting off, right?"

She looked away and pinched the bridge of her nose before she nodded. "Yeah, I guess that's exactly what this is."

Good.
We were on the same page.

"Yeah, well, I think we should stop. It's been fun, but I think we've had enough. We should go back to being just friends. Don't you think?"

She didn't answer. Instead, she nodded, went to her suitcase to get some clothes, and started toward the bathroom for a shower. Her ass shook as she walked, and I forced myself to stay put.

"Shut the door on your way out," she called out, her voice echoing as she entered the bathroom.

And then she shut the bathroom door, shutting me out before I heard the shower turn on.

I'd gotten exactly what I wanted. She'd made it easy to walk away by basically walking away from me, as well. I should have been happy, but I wasn't. Instead, I felt a strange pain in my chest that I'd never felt before, and I left her room feeling like I'd just broken something priceless.

21

HOPE

The tears fell the minute the shower came on, and I pressed my palm over my mouth to quiet my broken cries. The room echoed with the sounds of the shower, but still, I was able to hear the sound of the hotel room door opening and closing when Chet left.

We'd spent the night together—touching and kissing—pushing each other over the edge so many times, I had lost count. He'd held me. He'd kissed me. He'd whispered sweet words in my ear as he entered me, sending my mind spiraling out of control with my emotions and feelings for him. I could still hear his words.

You're so incredible, Hope.

I can't get enough of you. I'll never get enough of you.

This is all I want. This is all I'll ever want.

Make it go away. Just make it all go away.

It was all said in the heat of the moment, but I'd fallen in love with him again. Giving myself to him mind, body, and heart without fear since I was pretty sure by the look in his eyes that he was feeling the same things.

He wasn't.

He'd made that clear when he climbed from my bed, dressed in a hurry, and suggested we just be friends.

How could I have been so stupid?

I was smarter when I was younger.

At least then, I'd walked away before he could break me. This time, I stayed for the storm, and the winds of his words had destroyed me, ripping me apart and scattering the debris of me all over.

I stood under the hot water until I was positive I was done crying. The last thing I needed was to meet the girls for breakfast with swollen, red eyes. They'd ask questions, and as weak as I felt, I wasn't sure I'd be able to hide my hurt anymore.

I dressed for the day without looking at the bed. I didn't want to think about everything we had done the night before. I didn't want to think about how he'd held me or the things he'd said in the heat of passion.

None of it mattered.

It was all lies.

Chet's specialty.

And I was dumb enough to fall for it this time.

I met the girls in the lobby, and we ate breakfast in the hotel restaurant to avoid going out in the Florida heat. Constance poked at her food, her face turning green as her morning sickness reared its ugly head.

She had yet to spill the beans, but I knew it wasn't going to be long before everyone knew. Even if she hadn't already told me, I would have known. It was apparent to me, but I knew what the symptoms were. I knew what she was feeling.

After breakfast, we hit the town and did some sightseeing. I was there, but I wasn't.

"Earth to Hope." Lena snapped her fingers in my face. "I asked you if you liked this."

She held up a shirt with a palm tree on the front.

I nodded. "It's cute."

I tried, but I wasn't really feeling it. I couldn't really focus enough to enjoy myself since all I could think about was Chet and his final words. Every time I thought about him, a fresh wave of hurt would move through me, and my eyes would water.

Thank God for dark sunglasses.

Constance was with Tiny and the guys, but I'd suggested the rest of us doing something different, so I didn't have to see Chet. I'd even suggested something girly like going to a salon, which I hated.

Once we got back to the hotel and collected ourselves after a long day in the Florida heat, we went to the venue to play our show.

Days passed, and I kept myself away from the boys ... away from Chet. Soon, we were playing our final show in Orlando before moving on to Atlanta, Georgia. The closer we got to South Carolina, the more the memories of the past and the worst day of my life bombarded me.

A few more stops in a few different cities, and I'd be home again.

I wasn't looking forward to our Charleston, South Carolina show, but at the same time, I was excited to be in familiar territory again. A few of my old friends were coming to the show, but I silently hoped that my parents didn't show. I'd run to California to get away from not only the memories but also to get away from them. I didn't even want to see their faces.

We played hard, making the crowd go wild, and sweat trickled over my skin as I beat the drums with all that I was. I took out my anger on my drums—my hurt—my everything. I'd always done that, which was the biggest reason I loved playing so much.

Chet wasn't on the side stage, but Tiny was, and I could tell by his love-struck, happy expression that Constance had finally told him that she was pregnant. They were perfect together, and they were going to be amazing parents. Being around babies wasn't easy for me, but I knew once their baby came, I'd spoil him or her rotten.

After the show, we had just enough time to get to the hotel, take a shower, get packed, and get back on the buses to pull out for Georgia. Once we settled on the bus and were headed north, I felt a tiny bit of relief flow through me.

At least when I was on the bus, I didn't have to worry about running into Chet. My heart was breaking, and I knew seeing his face again would only hurt more. I wasn't ready for that. I wasn't sure I'd ever be ready for that.

Atlanta was a busy place, and the girls were dressed and ready to hit the clubs almost as soon as we parked and settled in our hotel. On the other hand, I didn't want to leave the bus until it was time to go on the stage. Still, I dressed and let Lena curl my hair and apply my makeup.

The club we went to was called Sways. Purple velvet covered the VIP section, and an expensive chandelier hung in the center. Once we settled in VIP with our drinks, I sat in the corner and silently prayed the boys would choose another place to go for the night. I knew now that Constance had spilled the beans about the baby to Tiny, they would be staying in, but that didn't mean Finn, Zeke, and Chet would.

I didn't want to see him, so when he and the boys showed up, I instantly wanted to leave. I turned toward Mia and nudged her with my arm.

"I'm ready to head out. Are you girls planning to stay?"

She moved closer. "Just stay a little longer. We'll leave together in a bit."

I nodded, even though staying was the last thing I wanted to do.

Thankfully, Chet sat across the VIP from me, and even though I was relieved that he didn't look my way, I was still upset that he wasn't looking at me. I was a fucked-up mess. I wanted his attention, but I was thankful he wasn't giving it to me.

I sipped my drink, fiddling with the frayed ends of my denim skirt just to have something to keep my eyes on. The girls left me a few times to dance, and Finn slid my way and struck up a conversation.

"Thanks again for playing for us when Chet bailed," he said over the loud music.

I smiled. "You're welcome. It was fun playing with you guys."

"Well, we appreciate it. Plus, you kicked ass." He winked.

"Thanks."

Hearing praise from Finn would never get old. He knew music, and he knew great music when he heard it. He'd even called our next hit when he heard it the first time. A month later, that same song climbed to number one.

Once he turned away and began to talk to Zeke, I stood and made a run for the bathroom. The air in the club was too thick; the sweet smells of perfume and alcohol made me feel a bit sick.

I exited the VIP section, feeling relief the farther I got away from Chet, but just as I was about to step into the bathroom, a hand on my arm stopped me.

I pulled my arm away, ready to turn toward who I thought was Chet, but standing beside me and wearing a panty-melting smile was Reed from Savage Will. They had been on the Rock Across America tour with us, and we had spent the night flirting a few times, but nothing more ever came of it. I hadn't been in the right mindset to be with another man then.

Things were different now, though. I was freshly heart-broken, and I was ready and willing to do whatever it took to get over Chet.

"Hey, stranger," I said with a smile.

Reed was taller than most guys, and he knew he was good-looking. You could see it in his smug grin and the way he carried himself. He ran his fingers through this thick, dark hair, and his blue eyes settled on me.

"Hey, yourself." He smirked. "I was hoping I'd run into you when I found out you girls were touring with Blow Hole."

"You were, huh?"

He nodded, slowly moving me into a dark corner. "Yeah."

"And why's that?"

I was flirting, and it was fun. The heartbreak didn't burn so much when I used my energy to be attracted to another man. Maybe I was forcing myself a bit. Perhaps I was pushing myself.

My mom had once told me if I wanted to get over one man, I needed to get under another. Sure, my mother was a fucking wreck, but at this point, I was willing to do whatever it took to take the pain away.

"You look sexy tonight." He avoided the question and moved in for the kill.

"Just tonight?" I teased.

"Hell, no. You look sexy all the time." He leaned in close so I could hear him over the loud music. "But tonight, instead of jeans, you're wearing a short skirt, and I'm getting hard just imagining that you don't have any panties on under there."

His finger skimmed my bare shoulder before he bravely leaned over and pressed a kiss against the side of my neck.

I closed my eyes, hoping to feel anything even remotely close to desire, but instead, a wave of nausea moved over me, and I almost gagged.

What was wrong with me?

Reed was sexy and flirty. Most women would have fallen over themselves to be alone with him. I'd seen some try on several occasions when we were on tour together, but as much as I wanted to be into him, I wasn't.

I wasn't giving up, though. I reached out and snagged a waitress who was walking by with a tray of shots and took two from her tray, downing them both quickly.

Liquid courage.

I could do this as long as it was flowing through my veins.

"No need to imagine because I'm not," I said with a devious smile.

Reed grinned, his perfect white teeth shining in the black lights of the club. "I think I'd like to see that."

"I think I'd like to show you."

His expression went serious, and he looked around the room before he slipped his fingers between mine and pulled me across the dance floor toward the exit. I swallowed against my nerves and followed him, his hand feeling too hot and heavy in mine.

My heart was hammering inside my chest, and anxiety moved over me. I'd only ever been with one man. Sure, I'd flirted and played. I'd even taken some to be alone to make the girls think I was sleeping with them, but this time, I wasn't going to pretend. This time, I was actually going to go through with it.

The closer we got to the door, the more anxious I became. I couldn't go through with it, and I had until we reached the door to find a damn good reason to change my mind. I looked around for the girls, hoping they would stop me, but they were nowhere to be seen.

Just as we reached the door and I thought I was seconds away from passing out, Chet was there. He looked at me; his brows pulled down in anger as his eyes left my face and landed on our latched hands.

"Hey, Chet, what's up, man?" Reed asked.

I moved to the side, tucking myself behind Reed's shoulder, so I didn't have to look at Chet.

"Nothing much, just hanging out." Chet's voice sounded different. There was an unfriendly manner about it.

"I didn't see you guys in VIP. If I had, I would have stopped to say hi."

Chet nodded, his eyes moving back to mine. "Yeah, we've been here for a while now. Where you headed?" he asked.

I closed my eyes, hoping that Reed would say anything that didn't make it sound like we were leaving the club to fuck, but luck wasn't on my side.

He tilted his head in my direction and grinned. "Just headed out for a little fun." He pulled me to his side and threw his large arm around my shoulder.

Chet's eyes didn't leave mine, and I wasn't sure, but I thought I saw a moment of pain flash.

"I can't let that happen, man," Chet said, surprising me.

"Oh, really? And why's that?" Reed asked.

I shook my head, telling Chet to let it go, but he wasn't having it.

"The girls sent me to grab you, Hope. They said something about needing to talk to you. You might want to head back to VIP and see what they want."

I felt like an even bigger idiot. There I was, thinking that Chet might be jealous and that he was stopping me from going with Reed because he wanted me instead, but that wasn't the case. He was merely doing the girls a favor by catching me before I could leave.

I really didn't want to go with Reed once I had time to think it over. Part of me was happy that he had handed me my out. But the other part of me was upset that Chet hadn't been upset about me sleeping with another guy. Just thinking about him with another woman made me upset. Life wasn't fair.

"Another time," I muttered in Reed's ear before placing a soft kiss on his cheek.

I turned away without even looking at Chet and made my way back to VIP. I fell onto the couch next to Mia and shook her knee.

"What's up?" I asked.

"What do you mean?"

"Chet said you girls wanted to talk to me."

She shook her head and took another swig from her drink. "Nope. He was mistaken. I haven't even talked to Chet."

I looked across VIP just in time to see Chet enter and take his seat across from me. His angry gaze dug into me from across the room while he nursed his beer.

I didn't know what the hell his game was, but I was pretty sure from that moment on, I wouldn't be playing it anymore.

"I'm getting out of here," I said, standing. "I'll take a cab. See y'all tomorrow."

And without even waiting for a reply from Mia, I left VIP and then left the club.

The hotel was ten minutes from the club, and once I was in my room, I stripped down and put on a T-shirt and a pair of shorts. I scrubbed the makeup from my face and piled my hair on top of my head.

I'd had a long day, and all I could think about was climbing into bed and going to sleep to stop thinking about all the bullshit. I just wanted to shut down for the night and hopefully wake up refreshed.

But that didn't happen.

As soon as I turned off the bathroom light, a knock sounded on my door. I sighed loudly, pressing my forehead against the doorframe of the bathroom. I wasn't sure who was on the other side, but I was hoping it was one of the girls and not Reed or, even worse, Chet.

Another knock sounded, and I moved to the door to look out the peephole, except whoever it was, was blocking the hole.

I rolled my eyes in aggravation before unlocking the door and throwing it open in anger.

Chet stood there, and the second my door opened, his expression went from angry to relieved.

"You're here," he said.

I crossed my arms, obviously annoyed with him.

"Where else would I be?"

He shrugged. "I thought maybe you'd be with Reed."

"I don't have time for this," I said, shutting the door in his face.

He caught the door with his palm, pushed it open, and strutted into my room, slamming my door behind him.

"What's your fucking problem, Hope?"

I chuckled sarcastically. "What's my problem? No. What's your problem?" I could feel my anger spiking. I moved to him and pressed my finger into his hard chest. "You're nothing to me. We're just friends, remember? You had no right to stop me from leaving with Reed, and it's none of your fucking business if I'm with him or not!"

He grabbed my hand and pulled me into him. The liquor on his breath was strong, and his eyes were glassy. I hadn't realized how drunk he was.

"It's my business who you fuck," he said, sounding deadly.

His cheeks went red, and the vein on the side of his neck throbbed, threatening to burst.

"You're delusional." I shook my head as I pulled away from him. "I'll fuck whoever I want."

"No," he spat, "you won't."

"You're drunk, Chet. Get out. Go back to your room and pass out."

He was on a whole other level at this point. I didn't know who the fuck he thought he was coming into my room and telling me who I could and couldn't fuck, but that shit didn't fly with me one bit.

I pushed away from him and turned to open the door, but he moved behind me, pinning me to the wall and pressing his hard body into my back.

"You're mine," he growled.

His hand went into the hair at the back of my head and tugged.

"Fuck you," I snapped.

"Fine."

He spun me around, the room spinning with the drinks I'd had earlier, and before I could speak, his lips crashed onto mine. It was rough, his teeth nipping at my lips until I was sure I tasted blood. I didn't kiss him back. I couldn't keep doing this back and forth shit with him. Instead, I pushed at his chest and fought his hold.

Finally, I was able to push him back. I slapped him. My palm smashed against his face, shifting his head with a loud smack.

His hand went to his wounded cheek, but instead of anger, he grinned.

"Damn, I love it when you get rough."

Again, he pressed his body into mine, pinning me to the wall and trapping my hands above my head.

"Let me go, Chet. I'm not playing these bullshit games with you anymore."

His eyes cleared when he looked down at me.

"Playing? You think I'm fucking playing? You think this is fun for me? It's not. I'm in fucking agony because of you. I know I need to stay away, but I can't get enough of you. And seeing you with Reed tonight made me fly off the fucking hinges. Just the thought of another man touching you makes me crazy."

He rested his forehead against mine and took a deep breath.

"I've never been this way with a woman before. I've never felt jealousy like this. I fucking hate it, but I know one thing."

I swallowed hard, still not believing the words he was saying.

"And what's that?"

"I know I need you. You make it all go away, Hope. Please, just make it all go away."

And then he was kissing me again, except this time I couldn't control myself, and I kissed him back. He released my hands, and I put them around his neck, pulling him to me and taking everything he had to offer.

And when he bent me over the side of the bed, ripped my shorts down my thighs, and fucked me from behind, I didn't stop him. I knew it was wrong. I knew the following morning I'd hate myself, and I'd despise him, but my white flag was nothing but a tattered thread when it came to Chet, and no matter how many times I told myself no more, I couldn't get enough of the things he did to me.

I'd never get enough.

22

CHET

I woke the following day with Hope's arms wrapped around me. She was warm and soft, and her naked body pressed against mine in all the right places. I could definitely get used to waking up with her every morning, but it wasn't long before the pressure started building behind my eyes, and my headache made the room spin.

The painful reminder of why I needed to stay away from her began slamming through my mind. I'd set the limits. I'd said no more, yet seeing her with Reed had sent me on a spiral into the black. I'd lost it, and then I'd gone to her room and forced myself on her.

Sure, she liked it rough. Sure, we'd had some of the best sex I'd had in my entire life, but my actions were inexcusable ... especially since I was the one who had demanded we stop.

But I couldn't do it. I couldn't let Hope leave with him. Just the thought of his hands on her made me crazy. She was mine, but I couldn't claim her. I didn't have the right to keep any other man from claiming her. It was a fucked-up situation that I was sure was going to drive me insane.

She made a soft noise in her sleep and pressed into me, seeking the heat of my body. I'd never been in this kind of predicament. I'd never felt this way about anyone, and it really sucked that it was happening to me so close to the end of my life.

Part of me wanted to just come clean with Hope. Tell her that the end was near for me and explain that I couldn't do forever with anyone. Maybe then, she'd be okay with a short-lived situation. One where we could be together physically whenever we wanted but were exclusive to each other because of my irrational jealousy.

But the other part of me, the part who didn't want anyone to feel sorry for me or treat me any differently, decided that I wouldn't be telling her anything. As it was, I was going to have to tell the guys once the tour was over but not Hope. I didn't want her sympathy. I wanted her nails on my skin and my name on her lips when she came.

My heartbeat slammed pain against my skull with each beat, and suddenly, the dim light spilling into the room began to blur. I blinked, hoping to clear away the sleep that was glazing over my eyes, but the blurriness remained.

I stiffened, realizing the more I blinked, the blurrier the room became. The darkness moved in, circling until I was looking at the light through a very narrow tunnel. The tunnel closed and blurred with every blink until finally, everything went black.

I panicked, jumping from the bed and knocking over the bedside lamp with a loud crash. Pieces of glass littered the floor, digging into my bare feet as I paced beside the bed blindly.

"Chet?" Hope's voice broke through my panic. "Chet, what's wrong?"

I backed away from her voice until my back slammed into what I could only assume was the wall. It was cold against my spine, making me stiffen even more.

Then I felt her palms on my cheeks, bringing me crashing back down into the darkness.

"Breathe, Chet, just breathe," she said.

I wasn't breathing.

I sucked in a deep pull of oxygen, but still, I was completely blind.

"I can't …" I started to tell her I couldn't see, but then there would be so many questions. Questions I didn't want to answer.

"You can't what?"

I moved my head from side to side, blinking my eyes rapidly, hoping that my vision would return.

"Chet?"

"I can't see!" I blurted out. "I can't fucking see, Hope; just give me a minute!"

I felt terrible for yelling at her, but I was freaking the fuck out.

She went quiet, but I could still feel her heat next to me. My fingertips touched her soft skin when I reached out, and without even thinking, I pulled her to me and buried my face into the side of her neck to hide from the darkness.

Her arms went around me, her palms sliding down my back as she attempted to soothe me.

"Should I call someone?" she asked calmly.

"No. Don't call anyone. Don't tell anyone. Just hold me."

I wanted to pluck the words from the air as soon as they left my lips.

What kind of man was I turning out to be?

What kind of man begged a woman to hold him?

A weak one … that was what kind.

I was weak and blind … completely useless to Hope and everyone else.

I couldn't do this anymore. This was my reality check. This was the universe telling me it wasn't meant to be. I was lying in bed with Hope wrapped sweetly around me, thinking about spending the rest of whatever time I had with her, and then I go blind only seconds later.

No.

This wasn't happening.

I pulled away, breathing her in as I did, and I pressed the back of my head into the wall and squeezed my lids closed.

"Please tell me what's wrong with you, Chet. Whatever it is, I can help."

My head continued to beat. My panic refused to subside, but once I opened my eyes and the darkness was gone, I felt like I could breathe again. Hope stared back at me, her expression full of worry.

She was so beautiful. She was everything I ever wanted in a woman. For the first time in my life, I could see myself settling down the way the guys had, but that wasn't a possibility. I could never let it happen.

What kind of man would I be to put that on her?

"Nothing's wrong with me. I need to get out of here," I said, moving around the room and snatching up my discarded clothes.

"You can see again?" she asked hesitantly.

I nodded. "Yeah. I'm fine. Everything's fine. Don't mention this to anyone, okay?"

"Chet, I think …."

"No!" I cut her off. "Don't think. Just stay away from me, okay?"

She stared back at me with wide, pain-filled eyes, and my heart shattered.

"So now that the sun's up, we're back to that again?"

She crossed her arms over her naked breasts and rubbed at her arms.

It was the right thing to do. I was doing it for her. She'd understand that once I was dead, but until then, she'd hate me. I couldn't think about that, though. I had to think about her, and the last thing I wanted to do was hurt her, but there weren't any other options.

"Yeah, except this time I'm serious. Stay away from me, Hope. Please," I begged. "Just stay away from me."

She swallowed hard and nodded, her fingers digging into the skin of her arms. "Fine. I'll stay away from you. And you stay away from me."

Then she moved away and covered herself with the sheet from the bed like she was filthy. I hated myself at that moment.

"I'm sorry," I whispered as I finished pulling my boots on.

She nodded and looked away as she waited for me to leave.

I stood there, willing my feet to move, but I couldn't. Finally, with a migraine cutting through my skull, blurred vision, and a stomach full of guilt, I left her room.

I didn't look back. I didn't want to see the crushed expression on her face. This was the second time I'd pushed her away, and I could only hope that when I found myself in the same weak position pushing myself against her, she'd be hurt enough to kick my ass and make me leave.

I walked around for a week, waiting for someone to mention the incident in Hope's room. I waited for someone to ask why I'd gone blind, but Hope had apparently kept her word because no one said anything. Then again, people weren't really talking to me much anymore.

Ever since I'd missed the show and Hope had taken my place, the guys had been acting strangely. And now, Constance had joined their ranks. I didn't know what Hope was doing, but whatever it was, it was working because I didn't even see her anymore.

Somehow, she'd managed to evade me at every turn. And while that should have pleased me, I missed her. I wanted to see her face—hear her laughter—feel her skin against mine, but I knew she had the right idea, and staying away from each other was for the best.

And so that was the way my world was. I walked around with headaches while everyone around me secretly hated me and ignored me. It worked somehow, but I felt like shit for so many things.

We worked our way across Georgia, hit a few spots in Tennessee, and worked our way from Northern South Carolina to the coast. And when I stepped off the bus in North Charleston, South Carolina, the familiar humidity and smell brought back a past I longed for—a past that included my boys and me barely making it but having the time of our lives—a past that didn't include headaches and deadly tumors. I missed those days, and seeing all things familiar took me straight back to those times.

I inhaled a deep pull of Carolina air and felt a sense of home settle over me. Once the tour was over, and the guys were filled in, I was definitely running home to South Carolina to die. I wanted to be home when I left the world.

The North Charleston Coliseum was where the boys and I had gone to all our big concerts. Coming home and playing at that venue meant we'd really made it. I hoped all our old friends and fans who used to watch us play at The Pit would show up for the show. Seeing familiar faces would be amazing. I missed everyone and everything that South Carolina had to offer.

We stayed at the expensive hotel next to the Coliseum. I'd once tried to use the bathroom in the lobby while I camped out for Metallica tickets and was kicked out. Now, I smiled as I walked through the lobby, knowing we'd be staying on the top floors of the establishment.

Things had really changed in my world, and while I had more, I couldn't help but wish for the days when I camped out for tickets with friends and partied until the morning without a care in the world.

I settled in my room, tossing my things on the bed and jumping straight into the shower. I was more excited than I'd been in a while to go out for the night. I only hoped my headaches stayed away so I could enjoy a night in my hometown.

I met the guys in the lobby, and we waited for the Sirens to come down so we could go grab dinner in a group. I was nervous about seeing Hope again, but I think a week away was exactly what I needed to gain the control necessary to stay away from her.

I turned my head when the elevator door opened, and the girls stepped off, but from what I'd seen in the few seconds before I turned away, she looked edible. Her hair was up and messy, rainbow strands falling around her face. She was wearing a sleeveless tee with Marilyn Monroe on the front and black leather tights. She looked beyond amazing.

"Let's do this shit. I'm starving," Mia said.

I wanted to look at Hope. I wanted to memorize all the curves of her face and the many dark shades of her eyes, but I didn't. I kept my head turned and followed the guys out of the hotel.

We took two separate SUVs to the restaurant, and when we were seated, I sat on the same side of the table as her, but a few seats down, which meant I wasn't able to look at her. I did that on purpose since I didn't trust myself not to spend the entire meal staring at her.

I was becoming obsessed.

I didn't like it.

I poked at my food, sipping my sweet tea and missing South Carolina even more now that I was there. I looked around and smiled at the changes that had occurred. Our tour had been spent hanging out in restaurants and VIP sections, but there really was no party left. The guys were settled, and in a way, I was becoming settled, too.

I didn't have a woman in my life since I refused to let Hope get close to me, but in many ways, I was already a taken man. I hadn't touched another woman since Hope. I hadn't even looked at another woman. She was all I thought about, and I knew I was in love with her.

God was funny that way. I'd always known he was a jokester. He had to be, considering some of the crazy shit that had gone down over time in the world, but to make me, of all people, fall in love was too much. The fact that he'd waited until I was almost on my deathbed was what I deserved for all the sins and shit I'd pulled over the years.

Touché, God.

Touché.

Halfway through dinner, Hope stood and went to the bathroom. I nibbled on my chicken and waited for her to return, but she didn't. The minutes ticked by, prompting me to go and check on her.

I stood outside the ladies' room, ready to go in regardless of who was in there, but then the door opened, and a lady stepped out. With the door open, I could hear someone heaving inside the first stall, and I knew without seeing her that it was Hope.

I went into the bathroom and checked to ensure no other women were in the room. Peeking under the stall, I could see Hope's black tights and boots. I jumped when she gagged, and I could hear her getting sick again.

"Hope?"

The room went silent, and then I heard her sigh.

"Go away, Chet," she croaked.

"Are you okay?"

"I'm fine. Please just go away."

And then she was puking again, the awful sound echoing throughout the bathroom.

"Do you want me to go get one of the girls?"

She coughed. "No. Please, just leave."

Her voice was rough and broken as she choked and gagged. And then there was a loud thump. I bent over to look under the stall again and found her lying on the floor.

She'd passed out.

I went into freak-out mode, pulling at the stall door until I heard it crack and give way. Scooping her up, I rushed out of the bathroom and toward the restaurant's exit.

"Finn!" I called out in the direction of where we were seated. "Something's wrong with Hope!"

I didn't wait for a response.

Once outside, I pulled out my phone and called nine-one-one.

"What's going on?" Lena appeared at my side, breathing hard with wide, shocked eyes.

"She passed out," I said out of breath.

It was then that I realized everyone was circling around me. I held Hope close as I yelled into the phone that my girlfriend had passed out and we needed an ambulance.

I was sure I was overreacting, but I didn't care. Something was wrong. First, she was sick, and then, she'd passed out. I hadn't even realized I'd referred to her as my girlfriend until I saw Finn grinning down at me.

I was definitely overreacting.

No sooner than the operator told me the EMS was on the way did she come to. Her eyes skimmed my face in confusion.

"You scared me, Little Bird," I whispered so only she could hear me.

I wanted to touch my face to hers—feel her skin against mine—to know she was okay, but everyone was staring down at us.

It was then that she realized what was going on. Her nails dug into my skin as she clawed at my chest to get free. I held her close, refusing to relinquish my hold on her.

"Let me go, Chet. I'm fine."

But I couldn't let her go. It didn't matter how much she ripped at my skin; I needed to feel her close to me. I needed to know she was alive and okay.

The ambulance pulled in five minutes later. The parking lot filled with nosy people watching, prompting Hope to cuss me out even more. She had no problem playing on a stage in front of thousands, yet she hated all the attention on her.

"I'm not going to the hospital," she said adamantly. "Nothing is wrong with me."

"You are," I said.

Her eyes narrowed at me.

"I think you should, Hope," Mia said at her side as she patted her shoulder.

"I agree," Finn said.

It was only after Finn stated his opinion that Hope finally gave in. She stood, with a bit of help from Tiny and one of the EMTs, and slowly walked to the back of the ambulance.

Lena was at her side, climbing into the back of the ambulance before Hope had a chance to object. I moved to follow, fully planning to go with her, but she placed her palm against my chest and stopped me.

"No," she spat. "Stay away from me, Chet. Remember?"

She threw my words back in my face, effectively gouging out my heart and tossing it to the ground at her feet.

I opened my mouth to speak, to tell her I was an idiot for even suggesting that, but the words lodged in my throat.

I watched as the EMT closed the back doors and the ambulance pulled away from the curb.

"They'll take her to Medical University. Let's head that way," Tiny said, grabbing Constance's hand and walking toward the SUVs.

I followed, the rest of the Sirens and Zeke and Finn right behind me. I didn't speak. I couldn't. The worry was paralyzing, even though I was sure she was probably just dehydrated or overworked. I couldn't get the vision of her lying on the floor out of my head.

The waiting room was packed with broken bones, busted heads, and sick kids. My eyes scanned the space as the desire to run through the back rooms and find Hope sickened me.

My migraine cut through my brain, slicing at my nervous system and making me feel like I was seconds away from falling apart completely.

I rubbed at my temples in an attempt to gain some relief.

"Chet, I think it's time you tell me what's going on, man," Finn said at my side.

I looked around to make sure everyone else was occupied and not listening, and then I nodded, keeping my eyes on the doors separating the waiting room from the emergency rooms.

"I'm in love," I blurted. "And everything's fucked up."

Finn chuckled softly at my side.

"I figured as much. Love'll do that do you, bro. I'm assuming by your actions at the restaurant that Hope's the one who finally hooked you?"

I turned his way and took in his friendly expression.

I nodded.

"Yes, but I could never be with her."

He reached out and grabbed my shoulder, giving it a shake.

"Why not, man? I think it's great that you finally found a woman that can fuck you up. We all have. It's scary at first, but it's worth it, man. I'd love to see you settled down with a few kids. Living the minivan life and going to baseball games. Don't run from it. It'll catch you every time." He laughed.

It was time I came clean with Finn. It was time he understood all my reasons for everything. I could no longer hide behind jokes and the lies of drinking and drugs. I didn't want to lie to my best friends anymore. I just wanted to end the tour, find a quiet place in South Carolina, and die peacefully.

"I'm dying, Finn," I whispered so the rest of the group wouldn't hear me.

I wasn't ready to confess to everyone all at once.

Finn's shoulders stiffened, and he turned in his seat.

"Excuse me?"

I smoothed my forehead, hoping to soothe the terrible migraine. I hadn't had a pain pill in hours, and I couldn't take one with the entire crew watching my every move.

"I said I'm dying," I repeated. "It's a brain tumor, and it's the reason I've been so crazy lately."

"How long have you known this?" he asked.

I shook my head, knowing when I told him he was going to be upset.

"I've known for a while."

Finn sighed at my side, running his hands over his shaved head.

"Why didn't you tell us, man? We're your brothers, and we'd do anything in the fucking world for you. You know that." He sighed and shook his head. "No. We'll go to the best doctors money can buy. You can beat this. I'm not worried." He shrugged.

He sat back in his chair and rested his hands on his lap.

I closed my eyes, feeling sick that I had to tell him the rest, but knowing it was important to get it all out.

"I've already gone to the best, Finn. They've given me six months to live. I'm sorry, man."

I couldn't look at him, but I felt the tension in his body. I felt the sadness, and it sickened me, knowing I was causing my brother so much pain.

"Six months? Have you discussed chemo? What about surgery? There have to be options, Chet. I refuse to believe the best doctors in the fucking world would just sit back and let you die!"

His voice was getting louder, drawing the attention of the rest of the group.

"It's complicated. If I only have a little bit of time left on this Earth, I want to live it happy. Chemo makes you sick and weak, and surgery has its risks. I won't do anything to keep me from playing the drums."

"Fuck the drums!" he bellowed.

Zeke and Tiny stood and started our way.

I tried to calm him. "Stop, Finn. Don't do this now, man. We'll talk about this later."

"Later? There isn't much of a later now, is there, Chet?"

I didn't answer.

I couldn't because he was right. I didn't have much time left, but I would make everything better before my grand exit.

I didn't look at him as I stood and left the waiting room. I could feel Tiny and Zeke's eyes on me as I left, but I needed to get out of there before Finn exploded. I understood him, and I knew he was hurting and scared. Hell, I was too. I understood he was lashing out, and I understood it was out of fear.

The automatic doors opened for me, and fresh air moved in. I stepped outside, sucking in as much oxygen as possible, but I didn't make it far before I leaned into the closest bush and got sick.

I thought I'd feel better once I came clean to my boys, but as it turned out, telling your best friend that you're dying didn't bring much relief. Instead, it made my headache worse, and the guilt in my gut thicken.

23

Hope

The ride to the hospital was short. I felt ridiculous for even going since I was sure I'd just eaten something bad, but I was willing to do anything to get away from Chet. I hated that it felt so good when he held me, and I wanted to be away from everything involving him.

More than anything, I despised him when he acted like he cared about me since I knew he didn't. Waking up in his arms was too much, but looking into his face and seeing his worried expression pushed me over the edge.

I wanted to scream at him for pretending. I was sick and tired of his back and forth games, and I was done playing them. I didn't want him near me, even if his touch made me feel better than I had since the last time he'd left my room. I was exhausted with the heartache and the never-ending thoughts, but I couldn't make them stop.

So I climbed into the ambulance and let them take me away.

It didn't take long for them to put me in a room, and once I settled, they sent me to the bathroom to piss in a cup. When I returned, they checked my vitals. My blood pressure was slightly high, but the nurses didn't seem concerned. I knew it was because I was under so much stress.

"So what happened?" Lena asked once the room cleared, and we finally found ourselves alone.

"I'm not sure. I just got sick. The next thing I knew, I was waking up in Chet's arms. He was probably just trying to cop a feel."

"I don't think so. He obviously cares about you, Hope. You should have seen him running through the restaurant with you in his arms. I've never seen a man so scared."

I shook my head. "No, he doesn't. Trust me, I know."

She opened her mouth to speak again, but the doctor entered with a friendly smile.

"How are you feeling, Ms. Iverson?"

She was older but not by very much. Her brown hair was pulled back in a neat bun, and her green eyes scanned my face in an honest manner.

"I'm feeling much better. I think I might have eaten something bad."

The doctor laughed. "I think it might be a little more than that."

"What do you mean?" I asked.

"There's something in your stomach making you sick, but it's not food," she answered.

Still, I wasn't getting it. I sat there staring back at her, confused.

"You're pregnant, Hope."

The room shifted around me, and even though I was sitting, I felt like I was going to fall to the floor. Lena turned my way, her eyes clashing with mine.

"Oh, my God, Hope," Lena said, a tiny smile tilting her lips. "First Constance, and now you. Holy shit."

Holy shit, indeed.

She was smiling, but there was absolutely nothing to smile about. This was the worst possible thing ever.

Silently, I prayed that the doctor would tell me that she was wrong and really I was dying from the West Nile virus or something equally fucked up. Anything ... anything but a baby. I couldn't make it. I'd never survive it again.

No.

"It's Chet's, isn't it?" Lena asked.

Again, the room shifted.

He could never know.

Never.

The doctor, realizing that my pregnancy was not a happy surprise, picked up her clipboard and started toward the door.

"I'll put together your discharge papers."

I nodded, too afraid to speak.

"Lena," I choked out once the doctor had left the room. "You can't tell anyone. Chet can't find out."

"But ..." she started.

"Don't speak a word of this," I interrupted her. "Promise me, Lena. Promise you won't say anything."

She nodded, biting her bottom lip nervously. "I won't say anything. Promise."

I sat back on the bed to stop the room from spinning, and it was then that the tears started. I never cried in front of anyone, but I couldn't stop them. Lena stared at me in shock, and I swiped at the tears pouring down my cheeks to hide them.

Pregnant.

I was pregnant.

How could I let this happen?

Hadn't I learned my lesson five years ago?

Consequences.

I'd known the consequences, and still, I'd let him enter me. I'd let him fuck me senseless without even thinking about protection.

I was on the pill, but being on tour meant missing some occasionally.

How could I be so stupid?

How could I make the same mistake twice?

The doctor returned thirty minutes later with my discharge papers, and I listened quietly as she went over a list of things I could do to help with my morning sickness. I zoned out as I signed my discharge papers and walked out.

I couldn't do it.

I couldn't go through this again.

I closed my eyes, and memories rammed into me like a bull. Memories that struck fear deep in my conscience, making my stomach roil with guilt and loss.

I was so young—clueless—and had no one to talk me through it. My mother was no kind of mother and called me a whore when I'd finally started to show and could no longer hide it.

My father had kicked me out for three weeks before getting drunk and welcoming me home again. Still, for months, I'd been alone in the world, feeling a baby move in my stomach and knowing I had no way to care for it and no one to help me.

I'd pushed for so long, after months of issues—high blood pressure—that required bed rest, which was hard considering my home life wasn't the best. I stayed with friends on the nights my parents were fucked up. I'd even slept in the back of my mom's shitty car once or twice.

I'd done all this while being pregnant. I'd done all this when I was supposed to be on bed rest with my feet up without a worry in the world. That didn't happen, though, and after two hours of pushing, I'd delivered a sleeping baby.

Stillborn.

Lifeless.

Dead.

There were no happy cries … no wiggly bundle of joy in my arms. Instead, I'd held her, and she was still. No breathing. No sound. I had cried for an hour before the nurses took her away. And at that moment, when I set my baby—my heart—in the arms of a stranger and watched them walk away, I died. I changed forever, and I'd never been the same.

I couldn't go through that again.

I wouldn't.

Needless to say, I panicked inside while trying to remain as completely composed as possible on the outside. I wouldn't break in front of everyone, but the second I was in my hotel room alone, I could let it all out. I was a wreck. I'd always been a wreck.

Everyone except Chet was waiting in the waiting room when I was released. I went to the group and accepted their hugs before telling them a lie.

"I had some bad chicken or something. The doctor says it will pass soon, and I should be well enough to play at our next show."

Lena shook her head at me, knowing that I was lying, but I knew I could trust her to keep my secret for a little while. At least until I figured out what I was going to do.

Finn wrapped his arm around my shoulders and kissed my temple. It was strange and out of character for Finn, but I tried not to overthink it. He was usually a nice guy, always making sure everyone was taken care of, and it felt good to be included in his group of people he gave a shit about.

"Quit putting strange things in your mouth, girl," Twiggy said, making the group and myself laugh.

"I will." I grinned.

We left the hospital and went into the parking lot. That was where we found Chet, leaning against one of the SUVs and looking pale and sick. He looked up when we got close, and his eyes connected with mine.

"Everything okay?" he asked.

I nodded. "Fucking awesome." Blowing him off, I turned to the girls. "Can we please go back to the hotel now?"

The ride back to the hotel was quiet, but Twiggy was dying to talk. She usually was, which meant the girls must have asked her to give me space.

"Girls, we'll talk later," I said to soothe the tension. "I just want to go to my room, get a shower, and sleep for a bit."

"That's completely understandable," Mia said as she patted my knee. "I bet you're exhausted, babe."

Panic ran through me, and my eyes flashed to Lena.

Had she told the girls?

She shook her head as if knowing what I was thinking, and I relaxed against the seat.

I couldn't get to my room fast enough. I practically ran down the hall from the elevator and shut the door behind me once I was inside my room. The lock caught, not allowing the door to close all the way, but I didn't care. Within seconds, the tears came, wracking me with sobs that hurt my chest. I fell to my bed and tucked my face against my knees. My tears dripped from my cheeks and ran down the front of my legs.

How was I going to do this?

Should I tell Chet?

Things were different. I wasn't young and stupid anymore. I was an adult ... one with a good job and plenty of money to take care of myself. I didn't need anything from Chet. Nothing was expected from him. I'd have to make sure he knew that before I told him ... *if* I told him.

My door opened as if I summoned him, and he walked in.

"Don't you know how to knock?"

He stood in the doorway before moving toward me, shutting the door behind him.

I held my hand out to stop him. "No, Chet, not now. I can't right now."

I couldn't be near him at the moment. I was already breaking. If he touched me, I'd crumble.

But he didn't listen to my request. Instead, he sat beside me and pulled me into his arms, holding me to his chest as I cried harder than I had in five years.

I was so weak when it came to him. So instead of pulling away, I buried myself in his chest and let it all go. I cried over the past and the loss of my baby. I cried over my current predicament, and then I cried even harder at how bleak my future was looking.

"Whatever it is, it's going to be okay, Blackbird. Everything's going to be okay," he whispered against my hair.

He didn't know what he was talking about. I didn't blame him for my last loss. He didn't even know about it. I blamed myself. I could have done more. I could have been healthier. If only I'd had a place to live and healthy food to eat, then maybe my baby would have lived, but she didn't, and now, I was scared to death I'd deliver another sleeping baby.

"It won't." I shook my head. "Nothing's ever going to be okay again."

He wiped at my tears, making me cry even harder with his attentiveness. I couldn't seem to stop them. The memories were hurting—the pain from all those years ago adding to my emotions—and the shock that I'd done it to myself all over again, knocking my sadness out of the park.

I'd gotten pregnant by a man who wanted nothing to do with me. We'd slept together several times, but already twice, he'd told me to go away. I knew if I told him about the pregnancy, he'd make a run for it.

Maybe that was the best way to rid myself of him and all the things he was capable of doing to me physically and emotionally.

"I need to tell you something," I said, leaning back and swiping at my tears.

He tucked wet strands behind my ears and let his thumbs linger over my cheeks.

"You can tell me anything."

How was it possible that Chet could be two men at once?

One minute, he was telling me to leave him alone, and the next, he was caressing me and telling me to trust him.

It was time to end this. It was time to blow him away. After pushing me away so much, it was time I returned the favor. Chet needed to leave me alone, and the best way to ensure that was to scare him with responsibility.

"I'm pregnant," I blurted.

His eyes went wide, and his mouth fell open. His fingertips, which were soft and caressing seconds before, fell from my face. He was pale, and I could see the anxiety slamming into him.

"Are ... are you sure?" he stuttered.

I nodded. "Yeah, I'm sure."

I should have known before the emergency room visit. My period was late, but I figured I was overworking myself on tour. I knew I was starting to feel sick, but I assumed I'd eaten something bad. During my first pregnancy, I never threw up once. It was different this time.

Chet stood, his hands tangled in the hair hanging in his eyes. The air escaping his lungs was loud as he began to hyperventilate. I couldn't keep this up. He looked like he was seconds away from passing out. That was the last thing I wanted him to do.

"You don't have to worry about this, Chet. If I decide to keep it, you won't need to do anything. We never have to speak again," I assured him.

He stopped pacing beside my bed, and his body went tense. Pain had seeped into his expression before the confusion swept in.

"If you decide to keep it? Why wouldn't you keep it?"

I looked away, swiping at my nose once again.

"I'm not sure I'm ready. I don't know that I'll ever be ready. I'm a single woman. I live a wild lifestyle. I wouldn't know how to care for a baby." I made as many excuses as I could.

"What about what I want?" he asked, surprising me. He sat beside me and grabbed my hand, squeezing it with his larger one. "I know I've been back and forth lately, but I swear I have my reasons, Hope. Don't take this baby away from me. Please." I didn't know he was capable of the emotion that broke his voice.

This wasn't what I expected. I thought he'd be halfway back to his room by now, running at the first chance I gave him, but instead, he was sitting beside me and begging me not to keep the baby from him.

"I don't understand. I thought you'd want an out. What are you saying, Chet?"

He lifted my hand, pressing a soft kiss to my palm. His eyes stayed on mine as if he was drinking me in.

"I'm saying let me fix us ... whatever we are. Let me fix it and make everything better. I'll take care of you, Hope. I'll take care of you and our baby. I'll stop everything—the drinking, the drugs. I'll do whatever it takes. Just, please ... give me a chance."

I pulled away, moving away from him to catch my breath. Everything was moving so fast—too fast if you asked me. I wasn't ready for the things he was offering, but I knew deep down it was what I wanted. It was what I'd always wanted from Chet. I just didn't want him to force himself into it because of a baby.

"Chet, just because I'm pregnant doesn't mean you have to ...."

He pulled me to him, stopping me from finishing my sentence. "Stop. It's not because you're pregnant. Although, knowing that my child is growing inside you has given me more than I've had in my entire life. I have a reason now."

His fingers sifted through my hair then he captured my cheeks in his palm.

"I haven't been able to stay away from you on this tour. I keep pushing you away because I know I can't be what you deserve, but I'd really like to try. If you give me a chance, I'll try to be the man you and our baby deserves."

Fresh tears rushed over my cheeks, collecting at my chin before bouncing onto the front of my shirt. His words were beautiful and filled me with hope I knew I shouldn't have, but I couldn't help myself. I couldn't help but feel like maybe, this time, it would be different. I could eat better and have a safe place to sleep.

"Let's just get through this tour," he said, capturing one of my tears with his thumb. "Then we'll figure this out. Okay?"

I nodded and sniffled.

"Okay."

24

CHET

The guys said nothing on the way back to the hotel, even though Finn didn't take his eyes off me. He was stewing, and I knew it wouldn't be long before he exploded. I understood Finn, and I knew he was hurting and upset that I hadn't come to him sooner, but I couldn't do anything about that.

Either way, I knew the night was going to be a long one. Finn would tell the guys, and they would spend the night trying to talk me into surgery. But before that happened, I wanted to see Hope. I wanted to make sure she was okay.

I leaped from the SUV and went straight to Hope's room. Finn's voice sounded behind me, trying to stop me, but I kept moving. If I stopped and they started talking, I'd never make it to her room. I didn't know then that she would shift my world ... that she would change everything I was thinking when it came to dying and having surgery.

A baby.

Hope was pregnant.

I left her room an hour later in complete and total shock. I had to rethink everything. I had to prioritize. Things that seemed so crucial before slipped to the back of my mind, and being a dependable father moved to the forefront.

A father.

I was going to be a father.

Nothing else mattered from that point on.

Finn's room was at the opposite end of the hall, and when I entered, Tiny and Zeke were already there with Finn waiting for me. Zeke stood and pulled me into a hug the minute I walked into the room.

"Fuck, man, you should've told us," he said, his words broken and serious.

"I know. I'm sorry."

Tiny's large hand grabbed my shoulder and squeezed. "We'll fight this shit with you, bro. Whatever we need to do, we'll do it."

I pulled back and sat on the bed.

"So, what's the plan?" Finn asked.

"I'm going to have the surgery. Fuck the risks."

Finn shook his head and ran his hands over his face. All three were stressed out. Zeke and Finn had been on the road for almost two months without seeing their wives and kids, and Tiny was still dealing with his addiction issues. Putting more on them was the last thing I wanted to do, which had a lot to do with why I kept my mouth shut, but the cat was now out of the bag.

"I thought you said no to surgery?" Finn asked.

His calm exterior surprised me, considering how close to exploding he'd been earlier. I guess he'd gotten his explosion over while I was in the room with Hope. That was probably how Zeke and Tiny knew about the tumor.

"Yeah, well, things change."

Finn stood and began pacing the way he did when he was worried. I hated myself for worrying him, and silently, I wished that I hadn't told them about my issues.

"What could have changed in the last few hours, Chet? You were just telling me at the hospital that you were totally against surgery, and now, here you are, hours later, saying you're going to get the surgery."

I couldn't help myself; I smiled, thinking about the reasons I would risk it all to live.

Hope.

A baby.

A family.

The life I'd been dreaming about since I found out I was dying.

"Hope's pregnant."

Just saying it made me happy.

"Seriously?" Finn asked.

I nodded. "Seriously."

Finn pulled me from the bed and into a hug. "Fuck, man, congratulations."

"Wait," Zeke said, looking confused. "You and Hope?"

I pulled out of Finn's hug and nodded. "Yeah."

Zeke laughed. "That's fucking awesome, man. Congrats."

"Looks like we're both going to be dads," Tiny said, shaking my hand.

I closed my eyes and memorized the moment since I knew it was going to be one of the happiest in my life.

"So, when do you think the surgery will happen?" Finn asked. "We'll cancel the rest of the tour and go back to California tomorrow."

I shook my head. "No. I have time. The headaches have been a bitch, but the tour is almost over. Let's finish, and I'll schedule the surgery as soon as we get home."

"I don't know, man. Maybe we should just skip the rest of the shows."

I shook my head. "This could be my last tour, Finn. Let me finish it, man."

Finn swallowed, his eyes going sad as he nodded in agreement.

Things were looking up. Sure, I still had the headaches, and my vision would go blurry, but none of that mattered. All that mattered was that Hope was healthy and happy, and as soon as we got home, I was having the tumors removed.

I didn't care what I lost—if I were blind for the rest of my life or if I never picked up another drumstick—at least I'd be alive to hold my kid. I'd be alive to take care of Hope and build a life with her. Nothing else mattered.

We brought the North Charleston Coliseum down. We played harder than at any other show because we knew our family and friends were in the crowd. Familiar faces littered the front rows, and Finn's mom and her new husband stood on the side stage wearing happy smiles.

I could hardly wait until the show was over. Finn's mom was making a big dinner for everyone, and I could already taste her fried chicken. I hadn't had any decent home-cooked food since we left for California, and my stomach was growling just thinking about eating later.

I stood on the side stage while the Sirens played. My eyes stayed glued to Hope as she played. It was amazing to think that she was busy growing a baby while she sat at her set and played her heart out.

My baby.

Our baby.

My heart was so full. I'd never felt anything even remotely close to what I was feeling, but I knew I was the happiest I'd ever been in my entire life. Happier than I'd been when we signed our record deal. Happier than the day I bought my first drum set.

Nothing compared, and nothing ever would.

"I've never seen you smile so much," Tiny said at my side.

"I've never had a reason to smile this much."

And I hadn't.

My life was on the cusp of a major change, and while I should have been scared shitless by this change, I wasn't. I couldn't wait to get started on our new life when we settled back in California.

Our.

We.

Hope.

Once the show was over, we headed back to our hotels to get ready for an after-party at Finn's mom's house. It wasn't the place we practically grew up in, since buying his mom a new house in a nicer neighborhood had been the first thing Finn did after we signed our contract, but still, being with family and friends was perfection no matter where we were.

After showering and getting dressed, I went to Hope's room to pick her up. We were all riding together, but I wanted to walk down with her. Hell, I wanted to be near her at all times. It had been that way with her for a while, but now that things were settling into place, I knew we were going to be together.

I knocked on her door and waited for her to answer, but she never did.

"She's not there," Lena said when she exited her room.

She shoved her card key in her back pocket and ran her fingers through her hair to tame it.

"Where is she?"

Lena shrugged. "Don't know. She said she would meet us at Finn's mom's place."

I panicked.

This was Hope's old stomping grounds, too.

Could she be meeting up with someone?

She didn't need to be going through the city all alone. Things were different now. She wasn't just Hope Iverson; she was Hope, the drummer of one of the hottest bands out there right now. It could be dangerous.

"When did she leave?" I asked as I started toward the elevators.

"Like two minutes ago. If you hurry, you can catch her in the lobby."

At that, I ran. I ran past the elevators to the stairs, and I took the stairs two at a time. By the time I made it to the lobby, I was out of breath. I burst through the stairwell door, people turning my way, as I searched the lobby for her.

She wasn't there, but when I made it to the exit and rushed out into the Carolina humidity, I saw her just as she got into a taxi.

I pulled out my cell and cussed myself when I realized I didn't have her number. I hadn't needed it until now.

Scanning the parking lot, I saw another taxi parked across the way. I ran over, pulled open the door, and climbed in the back.

"Follow that taxi," I said, pointing at the car pulling away with my girl and baby in the back.

It was like something on an action flick, but the reality was I was overreacting. I couldn't help it, though. Things were going too good. I was waiting for something to come along and fuck everything up, and all I could picture was Hope going out alone and getting hurt.

I wouldn't be able to handle that.

The taxi driver followed close behind, and my heart slammed against my ribs the further we drove. I was anxious to jump out of the car and get in the taxi with her at every red light, but I was already feeling crazy for following her.

We drove for ten more minutes until finally, we turned into a large cemetery on the edge of the city. The rolling green grass was dotted with headstones. Flower arrangements of all colors and sizes marked most gravesites. A large white mausoleum stood tall at the back of the cemetery, and old oaks surrounded the land, closing the resting places in and separating them from the bustling city.

It was a beautiful place of peace and tranquility, and I felt like a total douche for following her to visit what I was sure was a family member or friend.

Her taxi parked, and she climbed from the backseat, leaving the car sitting on the side of the cemetery to wait.

"Park over there," I said, motioning to the opposite side of the grounds.

My taxi driver listened, driving in the opposite direction while still managing to keep me close enough to see Hope.

I sat in the back and watched as she walked through the cemetery, a single pink flower in her hand. She stopped in front of a particular headstone and kneeled to place the flower on the ground at its base.

For thirty minutes, I watched as she came apart, her shoulders shaking with her tears. She kissed her fingertips and pressed her fingers to the cold granite. I stayed glued to the seat, even though my heart screamed for me to go to her.

I wanted to hold her in her grief ... to wipe the tears from her cheeks. I wanted to be there for her always. Realization of just how much I'd changed in the last month moved over me, making me smile and warming my soul.

I was a man in love, plain and simple.

Finally, Hope left the gravesite she'd been crying over and climbed back into the taxi. They pulled away from and circled the cemetery before leaving the grounds.

"Stay here," I said to the taxi driver, as I slipped out of the backseat and started toward the grave where Hope had been.

The grass was soft beneath my boots, and I was careful to step around the graves. Cemeteries had always freaked me out. The thought of stepping over dead bodies was strange, but I pushed through, taking step after step until I was standing before the grave with the single pink flower on top.

My eyes scanned the headstone, and the breath rushed from my body, making the Earth tilt on its axis. I dropped to my knees, tears rushing to my eyes and blurring the engraved words.

It was a baby—a girl who was born and had died on the same day.

April 17th, 2011

Four. Seventeen. Eleven.

The exact numbers Hope had inked beneath her blackbird tattoo.

I reached out and ran my fingertips over the baby's name.

Angel Iverson Rhodes.

The baby had my last name.

Our night together five years ago came flashing back.

Hope had gotten pregnant, and the baby had died. The baby with my last name.

My last name.

Mine.

My baby.

The world turned cold. The skies turned black, and I broke, falling onto the grass and screaming in agony. I'd never felt pain so severe. I'd never broken so completely, but I knew an hour later, when I stood from the ground and made my way back to the taxi, I was a changed man.

Altered.

Broken.

Dead.

• • • ● ● • ● ● • •

I made a stop at the local tattoo parlor before going to Finn's mom's house. I couldn't think about food, and I wasn't sure I'd even be able to smile with my friends and family.

I craved a needle against my skin, stinging and burning. I craved anything that could hurt. I needed something to stab my pressure points and relieve the pain climbing throughout my soul.

Climbing into the chair, I told the artist what I wanted. And once his needles began to buzz, I closed my eyes and let him mark my body with a memory I never got to live. I let him mark me with the worst thing that ever happened to me that I never knew about.

And as he burned my skin with his ink, I closed my eyes and thought about the things that brought me happiness.

My children—the one I'd lost—and the one I was hoping to gain.

Hope—my Blackbird—my heart.

My world.

Not my drums.

Not my eyesight.

Just my love for the woman who'd always had me and my hope that our future would be a happy one.

25

HOPE

I **survived it.** I didn't think I would, but I did.

I visited my baby girl's grave, and I didn't die the way I always pictured I would. It was the first time I'd been there since the day of her funeral, which was really just me and a few of my friends holding me up. My mother had stood to the side smoking a cigarette, and my father had worn jeans with grease on them.

Needless to say, I took off for California a few days later with nothing but a bag of my personal belongings and a few outfits. California was as far as I could get from South Carolina without leaving the country, and I hadn't been back since.

Until today.

Going to her grave was the third hardest thing I ever had to do—the first being delivering a sleeping baby and the second being burying her—but I did it. And while it hurt as if her death was five days before and not years, I stayed and visited. I stayed and mourned her.

I placed a single pink rose below her tiny headstone etched with cherubs, which was purchased by a local church, and then I spent a while talking to her. I cried as I expressed my love for her. I promised to never forget her, and when I began to feel like I couldn't breathe, I placed a kiss on her headstone, told her I loved her and left.

Afterward, I had the taxi driver take me to the address that Finn gave me, but after sitting in the car and waiting for my eyes not to look like they were melting from my face, I decided to go back to my hotel room. I texted the girls once I was in my room and let them know I wasn't feeling great and was just going to order room service.

After showering, I pulled on a T-shirt and shorts, ordered room service, and got comfy in bed. I hadn't gotten sick much since going to the emergency room, but I think that was probably because I made sure to eat small snacks every few hours or so ... a trick Constance had taught me when I confessed to the girls that I was pregnant.

We were pulling out for Charlotte, North Carolina, in the morning, so I had all my things packed and ready, which meant once I ate something, I could crash and hopefully get some sleep. I felt like I hadn't had a decent night of sleep in weeks, but I wasn't complaining too much since most of those nights were spent with Chet.

A knock sounded on the door, and I climbed from the bed excited and ready to sink my teeth into the steak and baked potato I'd ordered, but when I opened the door, instead of a hotel staff member, Chet was standing on the other side.

He looked like shit. His clothes were disheveled, and he smelled as if he'd bathed in vodka. His eyes were rimmed in red, and his hair was chaotic as if he'd spent the night tugging on it.

He leaned against the door frame and rubbed his palms over his face.

"Can we talk?" he asked.

I didn't miss the slur in his voice. Obviously, he'd been drinking while at Finn's mom's house.

"Yeah, come on in."

I pulled the door open for him and stepped to the side. Once I shut the door, he surprised me when he fell to his knees in front of me, wrapped his arms around my waist, and buried his face in my stomach.

"I'm so sorry, Little Bird." His voice was muffled against my shirt. "I'm so sorry I wasn't there."

I pushed against his shoulders so he'd look up at me, and I could see his face. Tears filled his eyes before escaping down his cheeks.

I didn't know what to do. I'd never seen a man cry before, and Chet was the last person I expected it from.

"What are you talking about, Chet? Everything's fine. I'm fine."

I wiped his tears away with my thumbs before running my fingers across the stubble on his face.

"No." He shook his head. "I should've been there. Why didn't you tell me? I deserved to know about our daughter. Was I so bad, Hope? Was I terrible to you that night? Is that why you ran? Is that why you forgot about me?"

My body stiffened, and my breath lodged in my windpipe as I choked on nothing.

"What?" The word was whispered and broken.

How could he have known about Angel?

How did he find out?

"I followed you today. I was worried when I came to your room, and Lena told me you had left. I saw you at the cemetery, and when you left, I went to the grave to see who you were visiting."

He bent his head down, his forehead resting against my stomach. His shoulders shook with his sobs, prompting me to hold him against me.

He knew. He'd seen her headstone and her name with his last name. And I knew what he was feeling since I'd been feeling it for the last four years. Except for Chet, the hurt was fresh, and I could see it in his eyes when he looked up at me that he was broken on a whole new level.

I dropped to my knees in front of him and captured his cheeks in my palms.

"I'm sorry I didn't tell you. You didn't do anything wrong. I was young and scared, but I never forgot about you, Chet.

Not a day went by that I didn't think about you, but at the time, I didn't know what to do. I should've told you." I felt tears sting my eyes.

"What happened to her? Did she suffer?"

I shook my head.

"No. She was born sleeping." I sniffled. "She looked just like a tiny angel. She was the most beautiful thing I'd ever seen, but I promise you she didn't suffer."

"I want to be mad at you because I missed it. I never got to see her. But I can't be mad at you." Another tear slid down his cheek.

"Of course, you can be mad at me, Chet. I wouldn't expect anything less."

He shook his head. "No. I can't. I love you too much to be mad at you."

He was drunk. I could tell by the way he was talking and the laziness in his eyes, but still, my heart skipped a beat at his words.

He leaned into me, his eyes drooping with sleep, and I shook him to keep him from passing out.

"Come on," I said, tugging him into a standing position. "Let's get you to bed before you pass out on the floor."

He followed me to my bed before collapsing on the mattress. I untied his boots and pulled them off, tossing them in the corner. All the while, he lay there staring at the ceiling with a broken expression.

"You gave her my name," he muttered.

I stood above him, looking down into his dark, sad eyes.

"I did. She's your daughter."

The side of his mouth tilted up into a sad smile.

"Thank you for that. Thank you for giving her my name."

I nodded, not sure what to say and not sure if the words would even come out anyway.

I sat beside him on the bed and ran my fingers through his thick, wild locks while he stared up at me with stray tears slowly dripping down the sides of his face.

"You're so beautiful, Hope. I'm so glad I found you."

I smiled down at him, again unsure of how to respond. My fingers sifted through his hair, and he closed his eyes and sighed.

His palm settled over his heart, and he mumbled, "My little blackbirds."

He wasn't making any sense, but it wasn't long until he passed out; his breathing evened out, and his wounded expression relaxed and became peaceful.

I lay down beside him, stretching my body out against his side, and it was then that I noticed a bandage peeking out above the collar of his shirt. I tugged his collar down, exposing a spot on his chest covered with medical tape and a bandage.

Curiosity got the best of me, and I tugged at the edges of the bandage until I was able to see that he'd gotten a new tattoo right above his heart. Peeling the rest of the bandage away, I gasped when I saw the new artwork covering his skin.

He'd gotten a tattoo of a blackbird that was an exact match to my own. Beneath the blackbird was the same date I had beneath mine ... Angel's birthday and the day she died. But his tattoo was slightly different from mine because beneath his date were two smaller blackbirds, both with their wings expanded like they were ready for flight.

I smiled down at his new ink since I understood it. He'd tattooed me, Angel, and the new baby on his chest.

His family.

Our family.

And I knew no matter if he was drunk or not, when he'd told me he loved me, he'd meant it.

Leaning over him, I pressed my lips against his, and he moaned sweetly in his sleep.

"I love you, too, Chet," I whispered.

And as if he'd heard me, his mouth tilted up in a sleepy smile.

26

CHET

Hope was wrapped around me tightly, her face resting against my arm, and her soft breaths skimming the bare skin of my chest. At some point during the night, I'd lost my shirt, but I didn't remember taking it off. The last thing I remembered was lying in bed with her and telling her she was beautiful.

My phone lit up when I pressed the button on the side, and when I saw that we still had two hours before we pulled out, I yawned and wrapped my arm around Hope, pulling her closer to me.

A migraine was ripping at my brain, but she looked too comfortable, and I didn't want to move to take my pills and take the chance of waking her. Instead, I lay there while the beat of my heart smashed into my skull like usual.

I thought about the day before when I'd gone to the cemetery, and my heart sank again. I closed my eyes, remembering going to the tattoo parlor before finding the closest bar and drinking myself stupid. I felt terrible for skipping dinner at Finn's mom's house, but I'd texted him and let him know I wasn't feeling great. I wasn't; it was just for much different reasons than my tumors.

Memories of our conversation moved through my aching head, and I smiled sadly. It was out in the open. Our past had caught up with both of us, and we'd talked it through. I was sure I needed to know much more, but because I'd decided

205

to have the surgery, we'd have all the time to get to know each other's everything.

I wanted to know all about her. I wanted to know about her past—her parents—our daughter. I wanted to know what made her happy and what made her sad. And I smiled to myself, knowing that regardless if I lost my eyesight or my ability to play the drums, I had time to find out all the things I wanted to know.

And then a specific memory struck me. I'd told Hope I loved her, and if I wasn't mistaken, she'd told me she loved me, too.

My face ached as my smile grew. We had the real deal. I was as good as caught, and I knew it wouldn't be long before I was pulling father duties like the guys and calling home to my wife because I missed her and the kids.

My future had never looked so bright, and my heart had never been so full of happiness.

It was real.

And it was mine for the taking.

I wasn't going to let anything stop me from getting the life I never thought I'd have.

Hope moved, rolling onto her other side and turning her back to me. I leaned over her and pressed a kiss to the side of her neck, breathing her sweetness in and committing it to memory. Once the pain in my head grew, I climbed from the bed and went for my pain pills.

I was definitely having the surgery, and I didn't want to wait any longer to call Doctor Patel. I wanted to get in and have the surgery done as soon as possible, so I could put it all behind me and start a new life with my girl, but the time difference meant the doctor's office wasn't open yet. As soon as it was, I was calling and scheduling the surgery.

I tossed two pills into my mouth and swallowed some water to wash them down. My stomach growled loudly, and I patted at my abs, realizing I was freaking starving.

A tray sat next to the desk with leftovers, but I couldn't remember eating anything. Again, my stomach growled, so I pulled my shirt over my head and adjusted my clothes.

There was a Starbucks across the street, and I knew Hope loved them since I'd seen her and the girls walking around with Starbucks cups throughout the entire tour.

I smiled to myself, thinking about having coffee and muffins hot and ready for Hope when she woke. She had to eat, and so did my baby. It was the least I could do since I'd come to her hotel room a hot mess and drunk off my ass.

I'd cried in front of her, which was something I'd promised myself I'd never do in front of another human being, but she held me and soothed the pain as much as possible, considering.

We talked, and she'd opened up to me about Angel.

My mother was never nurturing, but I knew Hope was going to be an amazing mother. After the way she had taken care of me, I could only imagine how caring and loving she'd be toward our child.

So yes, my girl was getting coffee and muffins.

It was the least I could do for her.

I chuckled at myself for my thoughts. The man I was two months ago would have called me a kiss ass, and maybe I was, but at least the ass I was kissing was plump and gorgeous ... at least that ass was mine.

I pulled on my boots and tied them before going to the bed and giving Hope a kiss on the forehead.

"I love you, Little Bird," I whispered against her skin.

As if she'd heard me, she moved in her sleep, and a tiny smile pulled at her luscious lips.

I pushed a strand of purple from her eyes, grinned down at my girl, and walked away.

The hallway was empty, and when I pressed the button on the elevator, the door opened right away as if the lift was waiting for me.

There was a bakery in the lobby, and the entire room smelled like fresh muffins, but I figured if I was already on the bottom floor, I might as well run across the street and get Starbucks since I knew she preferred that.

A few of the crew members were outside the hotel, and I nodded to them as I passed. Morning traffic was already lined down the street with people going to work and starting their day. Horns blew. Music blared from the windows. And as I stepped from beneath the parking zone of the hotel, I slid my shades on to block out the early morning sun.

I waited for a car to pass and sprinted across three lanes between parked cars stuck in traffic to the concrete median. The other side of the street was going in the opposite direction, and the traffic wasn't at a standstill.

Three cars passed, and when I saw my chance to run across the next three lanes, I took it. My boots thumped against the asphalt as I cut across the first lane and then the second. I was halfway across the third when a horn blew so loudly I paused long enough to see a truck that I hadn't seen before coming directly at me.

The sound of his brakes filled the morning, and I moved to get out of the way, but I wasn't fast enough. A brick wall smashed into me, slamming into my side and tossing me into the air and onto the windshield of the truck.

The sound of glass smashing sounded before I was tossed again from the truck and back onto the asphalt. My back slammed onto the hard ground, my head snapping back and smashing into the blacktop, making the world go black.

Everything dissolved into nothing.

All sound ceased to exist.

And I went away.

I was no more.

27

HOPE

I was having a nightmare. This couldn't really be happening. Chet wasn't really being rushed into surgery on the verge of dying. He hadn't really been hit by a truck and tossed twenty feet away. It wasn't real. It couldn't be real.

"Someone tell me what the fuck is going on!" Finn yelled at the group of nurses rushing in and out through a set of doors we weren't allowed to enter.

An older nurse with gray hair stepped forward and placed her hand on Finn's arm. He was crazed, his eyes wide with worry and his breathing erratic.

"Sir, please calm down. You're scaring the other patients." She smiled sadly. "I promise once we have an update on Mr. Rhodes, I'll personally come out here and inform you."

"That's what the last nurse said an hour ago," Zeke muttered.

He looked as bad as Finn did, his shoulders stiff as he bit at his nails. Obviously, the boys weren't taking this well.

We'd been at the hospital for two hours, and still, we hadn't heard anything. We didn't know if Chet was dead or alive. We just knew the emergency workers had been doing CPR as they rushed him into the back of an ambulance.

"How you holding up?" Tiny asked, placing his large hands on my shoulders.

I hadn't really spoken since we arrived at the hospital. I couldn't. Every time I tried, my words would get stuck in my throat, and tears would rush to my eyes.

I couldn't lose him now. Not when we'd finally come to a conclusion on what we were doing. Not when we'd confessed our love to each other, and definitely not when we had a child coming into the world.

I hadn't even had my first appointment yet. I had no idea when the baby was coming. I only knew I wanted Chet there when it happened. I wanted him in my life.

Always.

Finn stood when another rush of hospital workers came rushing through the doors. They strutted past us, laughing as if my world wasn't crumbling ... as if the man I loved wasn't possibly dead or dying somewhere in the hospital.

"I can't believe this shit," Finn growled, falling back into his seat.

He'd already made a call to his wife, and Zeke had called his, as well. As far as I knew, the girls were getting on planes and rushing to South Carolina, children in tow.

"It's going to be okay, Hope," Lena said, patting the top of my hand.

I nodded but didn't look her way.

I was sitting in the most uncomfortable chair known to man, and I had been for two hours. I hadn't thought to move. Instead, I sat there, staring straight ahead with my hands resting on the armrests.

I hadn't cried yet, even though the tears had been pressing against the back of my eyes for hours. I'd spent the last two hours choking on my emotions and feeling like my heart was beating out of my chest.

"The family of Chet Rhodes," someone called out, and I turned to see a doctor standing at the side of the room reading over a clipboard.

Finn stood and started toward the doctor, and the guys followed. My legs tingled when I stood on shaking knees and started toward the group.

"I'm his brother," Finn said in a tone that refused argument.

The doctor looked up at Finn from beneath his black-framed glasses and nodded even though I was sure he knew Finn wasn't Chet's brother. Chet didn't have any siblings as far as I knew, and from what I'd heard Finn saying, his parents had left him hanging years before. Finn and the boys really were the closest thing Chet had to a family.

My heart squeezed in my chest just thinking about the family we were growing together.

He needed to be there for that. He needed to see his child and experience a loving family. I wanted it for myself, and I wanted it for him.

"Is he alive?" Zeke asked, not waiting for the doctor to speak.

Again, the doctor nodded. "He is, but it was touch and go. He had a major brain bleed, and while we were trying to stop the bleeding, we removed a tumor that was partially blocking an artery ...."

The doctor continued to speak, but I zoned out at the word tumor. Chet had a tumor.

Had he known he had a tumor?

I would think that if something were in his brain partially blocking an artery, he would have felt it.

"He's on life support right now, but time will tell whether he'll pull through and make a full recovery. We won't know much until the swelling around his brain goes down. He may never wake up, but if he does, there's a chance he might be blind or have physical disabilities."

I stayed glued to the spot even after the doctor left our side.

Chet was in intensive care on life support. He had swelling on his brain, a broken arm, broken ribs, and they'd removed two tumors. He wasn't going to make it, and everyone around me knew it. No one was saying it, but we all knew Chet wasn't ever going to wake up.

"Hope?" Finn's voice broke through my thoughts.

I turned to face him, but I couldn't speak. I knew once I said anything, the dam would break, and the tears would never stop.

I listened as Finn explained that Chet was aware of the tumors. The doctor had given him six months to live, and Chet wasn't going to fight.

Until me.

Until the baby.

Because of me, he was scheduling surgery as soon as we got back to California.

Chet's past actions suddenly started to make sense. His confusion in the hallway in Vegas and the sudden blindness in my room. His back and forth come and go craziness. He was pushing me away because he knew he wasn't going to live much longer.

It all made sense.

I sat in my chair and finally let the tears escape my eyes. They rushed down my cheeks and slid from my chin. I swiped at them, embarrassed that I was crying in the middle of a group of people, but I couldn't hold it back any longer.

Chet might never wake up, and I'd barely had the chance to tell him how much he meant to me. I'd only told him once that I loved him, and I wasn't sure he'd heard me.

If he woke up, I'd tell him. I'd express my feelings for him so loudly that when I was done, he'd have no doubts in his mind about how I felt about him.

I loved him.

I needed him.

Our baby needed him.

He had to wake up.

And if he did, and he had any issues whatsoever, I'd take care of him.

• • • ● •❚● • ● •• •

A week went by, and I spent every second at his bedside. I ate when I could, and I slept slumped over the side of his bed. I got to know the nurses, and they got to know me, finding out at some point that I was expecting. From that point on, they brought me treats and became more like friends.

The rest of the Bad Intentions tour was canceled, and the girls came and visited me as much as they could until it was time for them to fly back to California. I missed them, but I understood they couldn't stick around Charleston forever.

Constance stayed behind with Tiny, and every day around lunchtime, they would show up to relieve me so that I could go eat. I wanted someone there at all times in case he woke up, which meant if no one came in, I didn't leave.

Finn's wife, Faith, came, and so did Patience, Zeke's wife, but they didn't stay long. As far as Finn and Zeke were concerned, they visited more than anyone else, coming in at all hours since they'd gotten rooms at the closest hotel. The boys loved Chet. They were his family, and I'd be forever grateful to them for being there when I felt seconds away from cracking.

"You need to eat some dinner," Finn said, making me jerk. I hadn't expected anyone so late. "Sorry. I didn't mean to scare you."

He sat in the chair across the room and stretched out his long legs.

"Any changes?" he asked.

I shook my head.

There hadn't been any changes from the beginning. It was the same thing all day, every day. The same slow beeping of his heart monitor ... the same in and out of the respirator. It was starting to get to me. I was slowly breaking down, even though I knew I needed to be strong for him.

"He's going to make it out of this, Hope. If you could've seen the look on his face when he told me he was going to be a father." He chuckled sadly to himself. "All I know is there's no way in hell Chet's going to miss the birth of his child. He just needs time. His body needs time. Just have faith."

"I really hope you're right." My voice cracked from being unused. "I just got him, Finn. I can't lose him."

Finn nodded. "I know, but you won't. He's not going anywhere."

I smiled warmly at Finn, feeling a brotherly connection I'd never experienced with anyone before.

"Go eat. You're growing a baby in there, girl." He smiled.

"Okay," I agreed, standing and stretching my back.

Hospital cafeteria food wasn't as terrible as everyone claimed. I'd eaten breakfast, lunch, and dinner for a week. Still, I was getting tired of the same walls.

The exact route to eat.

The same everything.

I wanted to run across the street to one of the fast-food places, but I was too afraid to leave the hospital.

What if in the few minutes that I was gone, he woke up? At least, when I went to the cafeteria, I was still close by. Across the street wasn't close by. I couldn't do it.

Another week passed, and Faith and Patience, Finn and Zeke's wives, took the kids and left for California. It was hard taking care of babies from a hotel room, and even though I knew Finn and Zeke hated to see them go, they stayed behind for Chet.

The guys visited constantly. Friends of Chet's and Finn's mom showed up in the waiting room area but weren't allowed to come inside his room.

Over the weeks, his room filled with flowers of all kinds, their smell filling the room and making the place feel more like home. I watched as they died and were replaced with more.

Fans.

Friends.

Friends who were like family.

Gifts and flowers came from all over the world.

I only wished he could see how loved he was.

I used Finn's hotel room to shower when I needed to, but it was the only time I left the hospital. And the showers were so fast I never felt completely clean.

The nurses set up a cot in Chet's room for me, but I still found myself slumped over the side of his bed, only being able to sleep as long as my hand was touching his. After a while, the sounds of his heart monitor and the in and out of his respirator lulled me to sleep.

It was life.

It would be life as long as Chet was in that bed unresponsive.

The doctors weren't hopeful, but they let us know that anything was possible.

Still, we stood by his side, and we waited. It was all we could do.

Three weeks. That was how long I sat at Chet's bedside. That was how long I lived out of a suitcase, showering in Finn's room and eating cafeteria food. Three weeks of lying by his side and hoping with all that I was that he would wake up.

It was the middle of the day, but I'd been so tired from the way I was living and being pregnant that I found I could sleep just about any time of the day as long as I had the blinds in Chet's room pulled closed.

I considered going to lie down on the cot the nurses had brought in for me, but I didn't. Instead, I slumped over Chet's arm, pressing my face against his warm skin, and slowly, I drifted off to sleep.

I didn't know how long I slept, but I woke to someone softly stroking my hair. I smiled in my sleep, feeling happy for the first time in weeks. But it wasn't until a single finger moved over my cheek that I realized Finn or Zeke would never touch me so intimately … They would never touch my skin with so much affection.

I sat up, pain shifting down my stiff back, and my eyes connected with Chet's. He was sitting up, his breathing tube removed, and he had a weak smile. I wasn't sure if I was dreaming, but it seemed real.

His feeble smile.

His glazed eyes.

The fragileness of his fingers as he touched me once again.

It was real.

Chet was awake … he was alive.

"Chet …" His name flew from my lips.

I was sure he'd disappear once I said his name. Or I'd wake up to find that nothing had changed, and I was still just sitting in a room with only the sounds of his heart monitor and respirator.

But that didn't happen.

Instead, his eyes widened, and his smile lifted as he tried once again to touch my face.

He was struggling to move his arms, but that didn't matter. All that mattered was he was awake, and he was smiling.

He tried to speak, but I moved closer, setting my finger against his lips and keeping him from struggling.

"It's okay. Don't speak," I said.

I wanted to rush out and get the doctors, but obviously, they'd already been in with him, seeing that his breathing tubes had been removed.

How had I slept through all of that?

Why did no one wake me?

I hadn't talked to any doctors yet to know what was going on; I only knew I wanted to take the time I had with Chet to let him know how much I loved him. I almost never had the chance to tell him again. I was going to take advantage of every second.

I moved closer, skimming the wrapped gauze around the top of his head with my fingers.

"You're awake," I stated the obvious.

Again, he grinned, his smile more vital as the minutes ticked by.

He struggled to move his free hand once again, as he tried to lift it to touch me. I helped him, raising his hand to my face and burying my cheek in his palm. His hand felt so warm ... so alive against my skin.

"Little Bird," he muttered, his voice rough and gritty. "I love you."

Tears flooded my eyes, and I smiled down at him.

"I love you, too, Chet. So much. I didn't think I'd ever be able to tell you that."

"But you did," he said, trying again to lift his head and failing. "You told me every day. I heard you say it every day. It was the reason I fought the fog so hard to get back to you."

I had told him every day how much I loved him ... how much I needed him, but I hadn't thought he could hear me.

"You heard me?"

The side of his mouth tilted into a grin that made him look like his old self. The man he was before a truck plowed into the side of him and almost took him away from us—before brain surgery and three weeks on life support—and I couldn't help but smile down at him.

"Every word," he whispered, flinching in pain. "And Little Bird?"

"Yeah?"

"Thank you for making me stay. Death tried to take me, but you held my hand. You kept me here."

And at that moment, I was glad I'd hardly ever left his side. If my touching him was what kept him from leaving us, then I'd touch him every day for the rest of my life.

EPILOGUE
CHET

Nothing was more stunning than my wife pregnant with our son—the swell of her stomach and the glow of her skin. I'd watched over the last seven months as her body matured, growing a life inside. Her beauty was growing more astounding every day.

She was amazing, graceful, and selfless. When I'd first left the hospital after the accident, I was a mess, but she'd basically moved into the condo with me, taking care of me better than any nurse could and making me fall in love with her more and more every day.

She fed me on the days when I couldn't lift my arms, and when I felt like giving up completely, which was often, she'd remind me of everything I had to lose and all the greatness that was headed my way.

Simply put, she was an incredible woman.

As soon as I could move my arms properly, and the doctor released me to drive, I'd gone straight to a jewelry store to buy her a ring. I couldn't go another second without knowing she was mine for the rest of my life, however long that might be.

I proposed on the beach. The sun had just gone down, and the evening was settling over the sand. And even though it was difficult, I knelt next to the water and asked her to spend the rest of her life with me. Her smile was radiant, and her tears were unexpected, but she'd said yes, making me the happiest man on Earth.

We were married a week later with only our adopted family in attendance. The boys stood at my side with smiles, and the girls stood by hers, holding back tears. It wasn't perfectly planned. Every detail wasn't thought out. There were no dresses and suits. There weren't even any flowers, but it's what worked for us. We weren't planned, and every day was unexpected with us. I wouldn't have had it any other way.

So, needless to say, I'd hit the lottery when it came to my soul mate. I'd watched her ripen, and my love for her grew as I watched her. I was in awe of the wonderful things she was capable of. She'd dealt with bouts of morning sickness, but she'd done so with a smile. Her tiny fingers and ankles would swell, and she'd be so tired that she could barely keep her eyes open, but still, she'd smile.

I was the luckiest man alive, and I showed her every chance I could. I massaged her legs and feet when she was exhausted. I made sure every craving she had was satisfied, and when she was uncomfortable, I ventured to the maternity stores alone and bought every kind of pillow known to man to prop her up.

It was the least I could do, considering everything she was doing. Nothing I could do would compare to the awesomeness of her, but I sure tried.

She rolled my way, struggling in her sleep to get comfortable with her expanding stomach, and I wrapped my arms around her, pulling her close as my palm lingered on her round stomach. A smile tugged at my lips when our son kicked against my hand.

I never thought I'd experience anything so perfect. I never thought I'd live long enough to feel so much happiness.

But I had.

Thanks to a truck slamming into me, my tumors were gone and had remained gone. Doctor Patel did an MRI every ninety days, and so far, so good. I'd almost died several times in the hours after the accident, but each time, they'd pull me back from the brink, and I'd stayed, knowing a woman was holding me to the Earth, and a baby was on the way who needed a father.

And when I woke and saw Hope at my side, I knew she was my reason. She'd always be my reason until Death finally succeeded, and I was no more.

The headaches were gone. I hadn't had one since my accident. And because I wasn't constantly high on pain pills or fighting the hammer inside my brain, I was able to truly appreciate my situation.

I was a man on the verge of greatness, and it had nothing to do with my drums ... it had nothing to do with the band or my job. The family I was growing was my legacy. My son was now my greatest achievement.

I leaned over and pressed a kiss against Hope's forehead, and sighed in contentment.

Life was good.

"Oh, my god!" Hope yelled, sitting straight up like she hadn't been asleep seconds before.

"What? What's wrong?"

She turned wide eyes my way, and the panic on her face sent me on edge.

"I think ..." she started before flipping the covers back and showing me a huge wet spot in our bed. "I think my water just broke."

I jumped from the bed and leaned over to help her from the wet sheets. We dressed, her occasionally grabbing her stomach in pain and making me crazy with the need to make it stop.

I wasn't going to make it. If I was having issues with the tiny bit of pain she was experiencing now, I knew I'd be out of my fucking mind once the actual labor started.

Tiny had warned me a few weeks before when Constance had delivered their son. He'd said it was the most gruesome and beautiful thing he'd ever seen. He said that Constance had screamed in pain, and it had killed him not to be able to do anything to help her.

I was about to experience that with Hope, and it scared the hell out of me.

We made sure we had everything, including the bag she'd had prepared for the last two weeks, and then I drove like a bat out of hell all the way to the hospital.

"Slow down, babe," Hope said, breathing through a contraction. "I'd like to make it there without getting into an accident."

I slowed down for her, but I cussed every red light that caught us and honked my horn at every dumbass that pulled out in front of me, going less than the speed limit.

By the time we pulled into the hospital, Hope was in so much pain she was having problems talking through her contractions. Things were moving so fast ... too fast, and the fear I was experiencing was paralyzing.

Once they had her in a room and hooked up to monitors, things only moved faster. Her body was primed and ready, and within the hour, she was pushing our son into the world.

She was beyond exhausted, her sweaty hair plastered to her face, and her cheeks flushed from one hell of a workout.

"I can't," she cried. "I can't do it."

She'd been pushing, and between each push, she'd fall back on the bed out of breath.

"You can do it, Little Bird," I said, pushing her hair from her face and pressing soft kisses around her temple. "You're doing so amazing. God, you're so amazing, Hope."

And then she sat up, hooked her arms behind her knees, and pushed once more, expelling our baby from her body in the most extraordinary way and solidifying my newest role on Earth.

Daddy.

We both held our breath as we waited for the baby to cry, and when the chaotic room filled with the tiny, broken cries of our son, I couldn't hold it back any longer.

I cried harder than I had in my entire life.

My shoulders shook with all the emotions I was feeling.

"You did it, baby," I cried into the side of Hope's neck. "You did it. I love you so much."

"I love you, too," she replied, her face still red from her overexertion.

She was crying, as well ... the pure happiness and joy on her face were contagious.

And when they settled our son into her arms, and I looked down at everything my future held, I knew nothing in my life would ever be as perfect as that moment.

Nothing.

I stood to the side and watched as my wife looked down at our baby and smiled. She cried over him while repeating how beautiful he was. I agreed. He was the most beautiful thing I'd ever seen.

"Do you want to hold him?" she asked.

I nodded, nervous and scared but ready to hold my baby boy in my arms and know that the moment was real.

She settled his small, delicate frame in my arms, and he was like a tiny ball of heat snuggling into my embrace. I held him close and kissed his baby-soft cheek.

"I love you, Aiden," I whispered.

And as I held my son and looked down into his soft face, I'd never been more grateful for my ability to see or move my arms, both things I'd ran the risk of losing.

"He's perfect," Hope said.

I looked up and let my eyes settle over the beauty who'd linked her life with mine. No words could describe the way she made me feel at that moment. No words could describe the depth of my love for her and our newborn son.

"You're perfect," I said, making her smile.

And she was. She was more than perfect.

• • • ● ● • ● ● • •

The boys and the Sirens showed up at the hospital an hour later. I'd called them before Hope started to push, but things progressed so quickly for her that they didn't make it before she delivered.

The room filled with our family, all of who'd brought flowers and balloons in honor of our newest member, and I stood to the side while everyone passed the baby around and went on and on about how perfect he was.

Of course, he was perfect ... he was ours.

"He looks just like you, man," Zeke said as he held Aiden in his arms.

Patience, his wife, stood at his side and smiled down at the bundle he was holding.

"He really does, dude," Finn agreed.

"Poor kid," Tiny joked.

I pushed at his shoulder and laughed.

Constance sat on the couch across the room with their newborn son in her arms, looking content.

I'd never felt so complete. I was a man with my own family surrounded by an even larger family—a family who was there from the beginning—a family I knew would be there until the end.

"My turn," Mia called out, coming forward to take Aiden from Zeke's hands.

She held him close and smiled down into his sweet face.

"He's so adorable, Hope." She sat him on the bed at Hope's feet and began to peel back the hospital blanket he was swaddled in. "I just want to see how tiny he is."

He kicked his wrinkled legs out and stretched.

"I think he needs his widdle diaper changed," she said.

Hope moved to sit up, but I pressed my palm to her shoulder.

"Lay back and relax, baby. I'll change him."

I had yet to do it, but it didn't look too hard.

I got a diaper from the stack and pulled the sides of the diaper he was wearing open to remove it. As soon as I pulled the diaper from his bottom, he peed all over me. The stream was high enough to go in my face, making the entire room burst out in laughter.

"Ah, man, he pissed right in your face." Finn laughed.

I covered his tiny junk with the new diaper, blocking his flow from hitting my face further, and I used the napkins Lena handed me to wipe my son's piss from my face. I couldn't help myself; I laughed.

"Well, one thing's for certain now." Zeke laughed.

"What's that?" I asked with a happy smile.

"Dude, he just pissed in your face. He's definitely your kid."

And I laughed harder because I couldn't have agreed more, and that was fine by me.

My boy was already a hell-raiser, and he'd just popped from his mother's womb. Hope and I would have hell to pay over the next eighteen years, and I was looking forward to every fucking second of it.

PLEASE consider leaving a review for HAVING HOPE!

From the bottom of my heart, thank you so much for reading! MWAH!

Stay up to date with my upcoming releases, reveals, teasers, and giveaways at www.tabathavargo.com

XOXO!

ALSO BY

THE BLOW HOLE BOYS SERIES
The Blow Hole Box Set
Finding Faith (Finn)
Convincing Constance (Tiny)
Having Hope (Chet)

THE CHUBBY GIRL CHRONICLES
On the Plus Side
Hot & Heavy
Thick & Thin

THE BLACK TRILOGY
Little Black Beginning
Little Black Book (New York Times Bestseller)
Little Black Break
The Little Black Boxset

THE SONS OF SINISTER SERIES
Shattered Skull
Dirty Saint
Joker's Wild
Ruthless Crow

STANDALONES
Slammer
Black Sheep

FOR MORE NFORMATION VISIT
WWW.TABATHAVARGO.COM

ABOUT TABATHA

Tabatha is a New York Times & USA Today Bestselling author, best known for her sexy adult romance Little Black Book.

Tabatha writes in all genres, including adult and new adult, and isn't afraid to venture into the dark side on occasion, as she proved with her dark, prison romance, Slammer. She's an avid reader of all things smutty and the writer of sexy stories featuring redeemable alpha bad boys and sweet, strong women.

Her other loves include her children, her loving, supportive husband, anything historical, and wind chimes. When she isn't writing, she's texting book ideas to herself.

Tabatha is represented by SBR Media. For inquiries regarding foreign rights, audio, and other media outlets, please contact Stephanie Phillips. stephanie@sbrmedia.com

ACKNOWLEDGEMENTS

This series has been years in the making, but I'm happy to announce it is finished. I want to say a big THANK YOU to everyone who read the Blow Hole series and loved my boys as much as I do. I put a lot of myself into my work, and there were times when I didn't think I'd make it through a few of these books, but I did. I can't say it enough... thank you for reading my work and hopefully loving it.

Also, thank you to my wonderful editor Jenny Sims from Editing4Indies. She makes this entire process easier, and I love working with her. I hand over a hot mess, and she gives me back gold. For that, I'm forever grateful. I adore you, sweet woman!

To my family: I miss a lot of time with you guys when I'm at work. The house isn't always clean, and dinner isn't always done, but you pick up the slack and allow me to escape into my books. Everything I do, I do it for you guys... period. Thank you for loving me no matter what and for holding me together when I feel like I'm falling apart.

To Matthew, you're my base, lover, and best friend. You're the reason I write such beautiful romance. You've taught me well. We've grown together and helped each other become what we are today. I thank God every day for giving me you, and I look forward to our future together. I love you, baby. Forever.

To my Angel: fly high, baby. And always know mommy loves you no matter where you are. I never got to hold you, but you'll forever be a part of my life and heart. See you when I get there.

And finally. to my beautiful sons, Asher and Jaxson. You are everything, therefore everything I do is for you. You are my world. Always.

To my readers, YOU ROCK! Thank you for all of your kind words. I love you all!

I really hope I didn't miss anyone, but if I did … THANK YOU!

For more information on brain tumors/cancer, please visit www.cancer.org

Thousands of women have suffered the loss of a baby either at birth or before. For more information on stillbirth babies and or miscarriages, please go to www.americanpregnancy.org

Don't suffer in silence.